FRESHMAN WISDOM

FRESHMAN WISDOM

Brandon Lee White

CHAPTER 1

"This movie is making me cry!" Emory hugs her red throw pillow and nestles herself deeper into my side, smooshing me against the couch's black leather arm.

"Wilson! I'm sorry Wilson!" Chuck's sobs blare over the TV as the volleyball hopelessly floats away with the ocean waves.

"Why are we even watching this?" She wipes her eyes on my shirt and looks up at me. "Are you crying too? You are! You are crying! Aww!"

I blink fast, trying to dry the moisture. "This isn't crying. Cast Away is an awesome movie! Tom Hanks! Come on! I can't believe you've never seen it."

"Lawson." Emory's ornery green eyes squint at me in judgement. "The only thing sadder than this movie is you not being able to admit that you cry when you watch it." She smacks me with her throw pillow, totally ignoring Chuck's breakdown in the background.

"Isn't this movie from the nineties or something?" Emory asks, playing with my left ear and ignoring the screen.

"Isn't it annoying when someone asks a bunch of questions

during a movie, especially during the important parts?"

Emory ignores me and pulls out her phone.

"Oh, come on!" I plead.

She turns her phone away from me and continues typing. "I need to know."

"Why do you always have to look up movie endings?"

Emory pauses. "They don't get back together in the end?"

"Well, no, but it still ends with… It ends good… Don't ruin it! Just *watch*!"

I pick at a hangnail on my middle finger. I'm nervous. I don't want to do this. I don't want to tell her.

Emory scrolls through her phone in obvious rebellion to my movie choice.

"Can we watch something else?" Emory protests. Her head suddenly shifts away from her phone to me. "Why are you acting weird?"

She catches scent of my awkwardness, my omission of the truth about us. She's right. I am acting weird. I don't want to tell her.

"Weird?" I reply, avoiding the inevitable.

"You're distant. You're not yourself, like you're somewhere else in your head." She leans in with her arms around my neck, hunting for my eyes that are still fixated on the movie.

"That's it!" She pops up decisively. "I'm pausing this movie until you tell me, because I love you."

I fidget in my seat, cracking my knuckles as I let out a

sigh.

"See. Fidgeting and sighing. I knew it." She flops on my lap. "What is it, Lawson?"

I am cornered. I want out, but there is nowhere to go. There is no more time left to stall. She is going to finally find out.

"Is it about high school next year? I know you said you want to start as JV quarterback in your freshman year."

"No. That's not it," I say, avoiding eye contact.

"Your mom? Is her depression getting worse—"

"No," I cut her off.

"Geez! You don't need to be a jerk! I'm just—"

"I'm moving."

Emory freezes, her expression slowly dies. They were the two words I'd been trying not to say.

My heart aches as she stares at me like she doesn't know me; she realizes she already lost me.

"Wha... what?" Emory stutters, slowly pulling away.

I almost reach for her to ask her to stay but change my mind.

My gaze drops to the floor. "Dad got a promotion in Kansas City, and we have to move. I'm sorry. I--"

"Lawson! *What?*"

"Dad got a promotion in Kansas City. So ...we're moving." I keep my gaze on the floor while cracking my knuckles.

"*When?* When are you moving?"

"Next month," I say reluctantly.

Emory turns her back to me.

"How long have you known?" She murmurs, sounding more angry than sad.

"One month."

She whips around and hits me on the chest with her hand. "You've known a whole month! Why didn't you tell me?"

"I—"

"And, why aren't you crying? Do you even care?" Her panic builds.

I lift my hands in surrender. Her mouth quivers and her eyes well up.

"I do care! I don't want to move. I don't want to leave you."

My explanation seems to pass through her. She cries harder.

I finally get up and reach for her, but she quickly backs away.

"It's not fair!" Emory says, hugging her arms and looking down at her feet. Her dark brown bangs fall over her freckled face as she begins fidgeting with the long silver necklace that dangles around her neck; that's what she always does when she tries not to cry.

"Why? Why? Why?" she whispers to herself turning away from me, her voice crackling more and more with each word.

I spin her around and pull her into me, giving her no

choice but to be held. "Hey." I grab her hands from her necklace. She pushes her face into my shirt. I don't know what to say, and I usually make things worse when I do.

"I'm sorry," I finally whisper. "I hate this, too. I want us to be normal as long as possible, which is why I didn't tell you. It's been tearing me up ever since I found out."

My cheek rests on top of her head. I feel the softness of her hair, the sweet familiar scent of her perfume. I want to say something, but nothing comes.

We stand in her basement, and, like in the movie, I want to pause my life. Maybe even start rewinding.

Emory lets go of my waist and heads for her room.

"Hey! Emory…"

"There's no point holding on to something you have to let go of."

My stomach flips over, but Emory seems to block out her emotions.

I start to follow.

"*No*! …I can't." she warns, running into her room and slamming the door.

This doesn't feel real, like at any moment a director will yell from the background, "Cut! Great acting everyone! Amazing drama!"

Instead, I'm alone.

I hear the clanking of dishes upstairs where her mom is probably oblivious to her adopted daughter's broken heart and the boy who could have been her son-in-law. Now, I'll just be another ex.

I look at the soft light coming from the crack underneath Emory's door, and then to the stairs leading up to the front door and out to the street back to my house.

Soft white light.

Clanking dishes.

Alone.

~ ~ ~ ~ ~

I throw my final things in my parents' car.

"I hate this. I hate this," I repeat in my head as I open the car door.

"I know this is hard, honey. It—"

"Linda," Dad cuts my mom off midsentence. "He doesn't want to talk about it."

"Okay, okay. I understand, Doug. It's just that I want everyone to know that this move is hard on us all, and I promise that when we get to Kansas City..." Mom trails on, but I block her out, because I know she is nervous and wants everyone to be happy. She always wants to fill silence, because it makes her feel better. Mom has always been this way, from what Dad tells me, and her appearance reflects that. At five feet five, a hundred-and-twenty-something pounds, with a soft voice that seems to only say, *'Please, I'm sorry, it's okay...'* she seems to disappear in her own fear. Dad, on the other hand, is quite opposite. Being over six feet tall, he is not afraid to raise his voice or stomp his size twelve shoe.

As we drive away, I imagine throwing myself out of the car and running back to her. But, it is useless. We are moving to Kansas City, and I can't stop that.

Kansas City, I think, looking out the window at the red and white turkey barns passing by. I like where we had lived in a small town in the middle of Missouri. I've never been to Kansas City. I've been to St. Louis, and I hated it. So, why would I like Kansas City? It is nearly as big, right? Without my permission, my thoughts drift back to Emory. I'm losing her. I haven't heard from her today. Maybe she blocked my number. She has always preferred to leave things unfinished than to face the sad ending. That's why she looks up movie endings, because the ending is too much for her to handle. It probably has to do with her being adopted.

I feel completely sick inside. The girl I love is probably bawling her eyes out in her room feeling completely abandoned all over again. We've been together for almost the entire eighth grade. Too bad we couldn't see this ending, but maybe it's better that way. Why do I feel so guilty? It's not my fault we're moving... it's Dad's fault.

I lean my head against the warm car window and see my reflection. If Dad had not gotten this promotion, we wouldn't have to move. Why does he need this promotion? Sure, we aren't rich, but we're not poor either. We're average like the people who live around us. I mean, 'lived' around us.

I finally blurt it out in a monotone: "Why do you need this promotion, Dad?"

Mom looks straight out the window, waiting for Dad's response.

Dad switches his hands on the wheel, taking a deep breath as he always does when he is getting ready to make an authoritative statement.

"This is a good thing, Lawson."

"Doesn't feel like it," I mutter.

"Yes, but it will, because this is a big step for all of us. You saw the pictures of our new house, almost twice as big, and a neighborhood pool—"

"How much money is enough?"

"Lawson," my mom whispers in a plea for peace.

I ignore her. "Maybe you can find a better job that pays more, and we can move again in a couple of years to have our own private pool!"

Usually, Dad would discipline me at a moment like this, but he knows that I kind of had a right to be mad, since he is taking away my friends, home, and happy future—all in 'my best interest,' of course.

After a few seconds, Dad continues, "I researched the school, and it has phenomenal reviews: plenty of opportunity—a great football and basketball team."

He wants to say more, or maybe he didn't, but he leaves it at that.

My pocket vibrates. I don't want to look. It is probably Emory pouring her heart out in a ten-page text that she'd been writing this whole time. Maybe it's about how she now hates me and my family and wishes that we hit a deer and flip into a ditch.

I look at my phone. It isn't Emory.

I'm filing child abuse charges on your parents and adopting you.

It's my friend, Bryan. I smirk. Finally, a good feeling.

I look at the empty seat next to me. Sometimes I wish I had a brother. I could really use one right now.

Kansas City: one hundred and eighty miles away. The green road sign taunts me. I think it also had said, *'You are leaving happiness forever.'* With each passing mile, the chasm grows. Our car is an armored vehicle transporting its detainee to a remote penitentiary against his will. If I could just reach the grenade in my bag, I could blow a hole out the back window and jump into Emory's Hummer for the getaway, but it's pointless because I don't have a grenade, and at fourteen, neither of us can drive.

I poke one rubber earbud in each ear and tip my hat over my eyes. The humming of the vehicle against the side of my head soothes me for a moment. It reminds me of a road trip my family took when I was nine-years-old. We drove all the way to Florida, which I would not wish on anyone. Well, Florida was cool, but the two things that kept my sanity were the DVD's and the gentle hum of the engine; the two most steady things in the vehicle.

"Lawson, we're here."

My eyes pop open. I must have fallen asleep. Mom looks at me with anticipation. "Let's check out your new house!"

Dad is already outside, scouting the exterior like one of those man trackers who assassinates strangers.

Brown.

The entire house is brown. It has a big front door with an overhang that peaks at the top. On one side is a three-car garage, and the other side has a large bay window. Up top are large bedroom windows, I'm guessing. I immediately fixate on the tan trimmed windows at the top right corner of the house.

"There's your bedroom, Lawson!" Dad proudly shouts from only ten feet away. He smiles, seeing that I'm already looking at it.

That's *not* my bedroom. My bedroom is 180 miles away. And, it's in the basement where I like it.

How weird. One minute your life is one way, and the next minute… it's brown.

Once inside, I notice the kitchen, dining room, sunroom, and living room are all connected in one big open space with the stairs in the middle.

"Hey, now we will be able to see what everyone is doing all the time! Cool!"

They didn't hear my sarcasm, because they are talking about the washer and dryer left behind by the former owners. I wonder who used to live here. It's weird that someone used to live in this house and probably for a long time. It's like a divorce—like making a vow with someone and dropping everything in a day, only to leave behind a ghost of memories and files of divorce papers. It's like saying, 'You're not good enough anymore,' and then breaking up with it, forcing it into a new relationship with some weirdos.

My phone vibrates again. It's Emory. Without reading it, I run upstairs to my new bedroom to get away from my parents. It's the one farthest down the hall. I slowly open the door, expecting the previous owner's kid to still be inside yelling at me: 'This is my room! My room! MY ROOM!' It's strange seeing rooms completely empty. It's one thing if it's a new house, because then it's like a new beginning. But when it's a used house and you can see signs of wear complete with occasional scuff marks on the walls, it's like something had been left behind, and it doesn't have the luxury of words to tell you about it. Maybe it was a scuff made in fun by a kid running with his toy, or maybe it was a bad scuff from a lamp being knocked over in a fight. Just from eyeballing it, though, I'd say it was a bad scuff.

The room is about fifteen by fifteen feet with closets on the left wall as you walk in. The cathedral ceiling is high with a large fan hanging at its peak. I survey my room. Sweet! I have my own bathroom. There's a sink, toilet, and shower. Perfect! Now, I only have to leave my room to eat. A mirror covers my entire bathroom wall. I probably look in the mirror too much, which I, no doubt, got from Mom. I got my dark brown hair and brown eyes from her, while Dad has dirty blond-colored hair and green eyes. Walking back into my new bedroom, I notice there's no curtains, so I stand looking out the window like in one of those horror movies where the little girl is standing there one second and disappears the next. Maybe that's what this all is: a horror movie that I'm dreaming about.

Our house sits higher than most of the homes in the subdivision. "Geez!" I say, noticing all the cookie-cutter houses lining the landscape. It's like a giant had been given a hundred Monopoly houses to line up and play life with. They are so close to each other compared to where we used to live out in the country. I mean, you could see our old neighbors but not hear their water running. This is ridiculous. Oh no, what if we have psychotic neighbors or the kind who have plastic smiles and say, 'Welcome to the neighborhood!' and then hand you an apple pie filled with 'suburban hemlock!' The sound of a train slowly passes through the trees, far off in the distance. I feel the warmth of the sun through the window as it shines in the midst of the blue sky, while one small white cloud floats all alone. This could have been one of those perfect days... but it isn't.

Sliding with my back down the wall, I come to rest on the carpeted floor and stare at the wall in front of me. I pull my phone out of my pocket and stop delaying the inevitable. The message is long. I don't want to read it.

Emory: *I can't believe this is happening. This is soooo stupid!!! Why did your dad have to move you? I REALLY miss you! The past nine months have been the best time of my life. No one has understood me like you. I don't want to be with anyone else.*

Emory is a lot like me. She can get worked up pretty easily. We fight a lot because we're both passionate. I mean, there were a few times when we wanted to kill each other, like the time when she literally rearranged my room and even threw away some of my things, because she said it needed a 'girl's touch.' I'm already kind of hypersensitive about people touching my stuff, and I guess she didn't know that. She thought it was cute and helpful. Well, I guess my blowing up and calling her controlling and a 'mom-girlfriend' had escalated everything. She isn't the screamer type like I am, but what she does is even worse. She gives you this little look that says, 'You are so stupid that I don't even have to say it.'

I bounce back to reality, staring at her message.

What do I write back? We aren't broken up, yet, but I know we have to, right?

I have to write something. There is kind of a rule I learned when texting girls that if they write a long message, you can't write a short message back. It looks lazy, or like you don't care. The only exception to that is if you say something sappy and romantic like, 'I love you,' or 'You're perfect,' or 'I miss you.' But, if I text, 'Yeah' or 'OK,' those are texts of death.

I call her.

It barely rings once.

"Hey."

I can tell she is crying by her raspy voice.

"Hey," I say back.

"Did you make it?"

"No, a deer hit our car, and it flipped in the ditch as karma for my family's crimes against humanity."

She doesn't laugh.

"Lawson..."

"Yeah?"

"I don't want to get over you. I—" She starts crying again.

"I don't want to get over you, either."

"It just hurts more, Lawson, when I do talk to you, but I would rather hurt more with you than without you."

Her silver necklace clinks between her fingers.

"I hate this. This is all my dad's fault." I stand up and start pacing. "He doesn't care about me or Mom or what we want. He said, 'it's for a better future for us,' but he never even asked me what kind of future I want. My *whole* life, he—"

"Stop. Stop. Stop. Stop," she whispers from the other end. "Look, I'm mad too, Lawson, but... not now." She pauses. "But I like knowing you care."

A horn honks outside.

"Lawson!" Mom shouts from the bottom of the staircase. "The U-Haul is here with our stuff. Come help us unpack!"

"You have to go, Lawson. Call me tonight."

"I feel so alone without you." I say, feeling my spirit seep out of my toenails and into the carpet in a puddle of tragedy.

"Me, too."

I spend the rest of the day pouting around my parents as I unpack our stuff and set up my room. That night, I lie in bed talking to Emory for probably three hours. We still don't mention anything about what we're actually going to do about us, but maybe we don't have to—yet. We fell asleep with our phones on speaker, and at 2 a.m., I wake up to the sound of her deep breathing on the other end.

Rolling to my side, I look at the phone. We have been on the phone for five hours, two of which we had been sleeping. I pick up the phone. "I love you, Emory." Her steady breathing makes me feel like she is right next to me.

Outside my window, the faint sound of a train rolls by.

Steady breathing.

Steady breathing.

Steady breathing.

CHAPTER 2

The smell of bacon...

Fan blades slowly spin above me as I rub my eyes. For a split second I forget where I am until reality smacks me like mean sister.

Oh, yeah...I moved.

The smell of bacon doesn't make up for it, but it sure helps.

Mom is definitely trying. It's hard to wake up to the smell of bacon and be mad. I throw on shorts and walk downstairs.

"Good morning, sweetie," Mom announces with a smile. "Happy Saturday! How did you sleep?"

"Mostly with resentment, but I'm glad you're making bacon." I give her a hug from behind as she flips the greasy goodness.

"Where's Dad?" I ask, grabbing my plate.

"He's scouting out the area and driving by your new school. You know, your father...he wants this all to work out."

"If we move back, Mom, I'll love him forever, and I'll spend twice as much time with crazy Grandpa."

She cocks her head, smiling. "The pool is open today, and it's going to be almost 100 degrees. Might be some kids your age there."

"Yeah," is all I can think of to say as I continue stuffing my mouth with cheesy eggs and bacon.

The rest of the morning, I put my room together while talking to Emory. Although we have been talking for hours, it doesn't seem to get us anywhere—just a bunch of feelings and questions but no answers. Our conversation ends, and realizing it is noon already, I put on my trunks and start walking to the pool.

"Man, it's hot."

All the beige-colored houses make me feel like I'm in *The Truman Show* with Jim Carrey, and everyone is waiting to reveal how this is all set up.

We had lived in the country with all the basic things. We weren't the Wrangler cowboy country type. We weren't farmers. We were, I don't know, normal—normal to me at least.

Now, I live in a cushy neighborhood with a private pool and perfectly green grass.

Walking up, I see about a dozen people in and around the pool: a grandma with her three grandchildren, a family with their kids, and one guy in his forties, reading a book.

Great! Just my kind of crowd! Oh… and a lifeguard! We have a lifeguard? Geez." Maybe that's normal around here, but where I used to live you only had lifeguards at the public pool. People had backyard pools with a parent occasionally peaking their head out to make sure the pool was still intact.

I walk in and lay my towel and phone on a lounge chair far, far away from everyone. The pool area is pristine with clear water, and I suddenly realize that I'm living in a rich neighborhood. I drop myself slowly into the deep end, because I'd rather not do my normal cannon ball and give off anything that says I'm a fun person to the kids. The water is a little cooler than bath water, which is how I like it. I'm a wimp when it comes to cold water. The end of July, like this, is just when it gets good. I swim around, trying to stay to myself. I can sense eyes glancing at me like, "Who is the new kid?" Maybe not. Maybe they don't even notice me. This is so strange. I've always had friends. Not anymore. I get out and lie down on my chair.

I start texting Emory when I hear someone sit down two chairs away. I look up to see that it's a guy about my age, or at least he seems to be. He is about my height and build, medium size with a slender frame. He looks at me from under light, scruffy brown hair and has a mole on his right cheek along with oversized ears and pointy nose. I don't know how to say this without being mean, which is a good indicator that I shouldn't say it, but you know how you can look at someone and automatically know they're not cool? I mean, you just know they aren't. I go back to texting.

"Hey, are you new here?"

Oh great, he's trying to be my friend. Why, why, why is this my life?

Looking up from my phone, I stare at him blankly to give the impression that I don't want to talk and then reply, "I've lived here all my life." Why not have a little fun? Besides, I don't even know this guy.

"Really?" he says with excitement, "Me, too! But, I have never seen you before. Where do you live?"

"I live in that house over there," as I quickly point to a random house across the street and go back to texting.

"Mr. Karigan's house?"

"Yup."

"Are you his nephew?"

"Nope."

He looks at me suspiciously. "I know him. He's single, and he doesn't have any kids."

"Well, I live in his basement, and he only lets me out when I'm a good boy."

"What?"

"I'm not allowed to say anymore. My master will get angry."

"You're kidding, right?"

"Shhh..." I slowly put my finger to my lips. "It's not safe to talk here."

He pops out of his chair and moves to the one right next to me.

"Hey, seriously, if you're in trouble at all, you need to tell someone. I've heard about this kind of stuff and—"

I couldn't keep from laughing. He leans away from me with a half-angry, half-embarrassed smile.

"My name is Lawson, and we just moved into that brown house—I mean, dark brown house, because I see that they're all… kind of… brown." I feel a little bad for playing him like that, but I needed a good laugh.

"Oh, okay," he says, trying to sound okay with the joke. "My name is Connor, and I live right next to the pool in that tan house with the green shutters."

"Well, nice to meet you, Connor." I wonder to myself how I can wrap up this little sweet conversation.

I look back at my phone.

"What grade are you in?" Connor asks.

This guy… You see, some people lack something called emotional intelligence, and they have trouble picking up on social cues.

"Um, freshman." I reply quickly, still looking at my phone.

"Me too! At Mill Valley High, right?"

"Yup."

"Oh, wow! Cool!" he says, starting to lose his composure from the thought of probably getting his first friend.

"Do you play sports?" he continues, not skipping a beat.

"Football and basketball."

"Neat, man! That's awesome! I don't play sports."

What a shocker. How can I end this?

"Hey, Connor, I'm sorry, man, but I just realized that I'm supposed to help my mom unpack some more things and set up the, uh, the kitchen plates and things."

"Oh, okay. Cool, man. I'll be here tomorrow. I'm here most days."

There goes my neighborhood pool.

"Okay. Well, then, see ya." I start walking toward the pool gate. Once outside, I look back to see Connor reclining in a lounge chair with a book.

I dial Emory. The phone rings and rings and rings… She doesn't pick up.

Approaching our house, I see Dad pulling into the drive-way in his gray Chevy Silverado. It's an older model, because we can't afford a new one. Well, maybe we can now. I don't know. Back where we used to live, Dad worked at the 7-Up plant and finally got promoted to a plant manager position.

Dad steps out of his truck wearing khaki shorts, a green polo, and black sunglasses.

"Lawson! Hanging out at the pool, huh? Meet any friends?"

"Nope," I reply, which isn't technically a lie.

"Listen. There is a lot around here. There's a Walmart about 10 minutes away and a little strip mall with some restaurants and shops. Oh, there are also some parks. Your school! Dude, your school is so cool!"

Whenever he is trying to be fun with me, he starts saying, 'Dude.'

"Beautiful football field. Big school. Remember, you will have about 300 students in your class..." he rattles on.

I don't know how I feel about that. My old school had 300 people total. I was definitely one of the popular kids at my old school, and I never had to try. I was never the new kid.

"That's cool, Dad," I say, trying my best to give him some sense of hope for our family.

"Hey, have you thought about how you want to make money this summer?"

"No, I haven't," I reply matter-of-factly.

"Okay, well, this week is a good time to figure that out." He gives me a thumbs-up. "Come on, let's go see how we can make this house more of a home."

Why do parents talk so weird?

Inside, Mom is unpacking her knickknacks and putting them in her display case. I know it's weird, but they actually make me happy, because I used to play with them when I was a kid until I broke one, and then they went on 'lockdown.' We unpack more things together and hang some pictures. After a couple hours of doing household chores, I figure it's time to give the pool another try.

I grab my towel once again and head out the door. As I

approach the pool, I don't see Connor anywhere in sight. I flop down on the same lounge chair from earlier. A forty-year-old woman splashes in the pool with her ten-year-old daughter. Looking at the lifeguard, the same one that had been there earlier, I guess she is probably in college. I suddenly think of the possibility of having a different girlfriend. The thought alone feels like I am already cheating, but maybe I should start thinking more realistically. I never cheated on Emory, but I've been told that I can be a flirt. Someone told me that I'm nice, good looking, and always willing to talk to any girl, so that, somehow, makes me flirty. I was told that the other guys won't talk to girls unless they like them.

Emory was, I mean is, my first serious girlfriend. I kind of had a girlfriend who was in eighth grade when I was in seventh grade, which made me feel basically awesome, but it only lasted like one month before she broke up with me in a text. Yeah. It's not that girls don't like me, they do. I'm just... picky. I don't want just any girl. I want a girl that I can respect. She can't just be some ditsy thing, but she does need to be nice. I don't want a push-over, but I also don't want a girl who is always trying to outdo me like a sister does. I want... maybe I want too much. Emory has some of those qualities, but... I don't know.

The sound of a toilet flushing in the distance breaks my daydream.

"Lawson, you're back!"

Nightmare.

Connor literally skips back over and flops in the chair next to me.

"You're still here?" I ask, trying to look and sound pleasantly surprised.

"Yeah, I was just getting ready to leave, but I can stay a bit," he replies in a chipper voice.

I look straight ahead, trying not to turn into a gorilla who throws chairs in front of the ten-year-old girl.

"Oh, I know what I was going to ask you," Connor announces, not missing a beat. "I was thinking. Well, I cut Mr. Karigan's yard. You know, the house you said that y—"

"Yeah, I know. What about him?" I ask, cutting him off to save time.

"Well, I cut his grass every Sunday, but I'm going to church camp for the next week, and I was wondering if you would want to cut it. I get paid $40. He even lets me use his mower to—"

"I'll do it!" I say, cutting him off again and thinking how perfect this timing is after talking to my dad.

"Oh, wow, awesome! Okay, well then, why don't we go over to his house now, so I can show you his mower and introduce you to him?"

"Wait," I say, realizing something. "He's not actually weird and crazy like I made up, is he?"

"Ha! No! Mr. Karigan is, like, the coolest guy in this

neighborhood, in my opinion at least. He's like my best friend even though he's in his thirties."

Oh no, not another Connor. What if he wants to make friends with my parents, and Connor is part of the package, and we start having game night devoid of any sarcasm?

Then again, I need the money.

"Okay, let's go."

Looking at Mr. Karigan's house, it doesn't seem to be quite as big as ours, but still…

"Why does he live here by himself?" I ask as we cross the street. "I mean, his house seems to be pretty big for only one person.

"Oh, umm…" Connor lowers his voice. "His, um, his wife and daughter died like five years ago in a car accident."

"What? Oh, my gosh!" I stop dead in my tracks, right in the middle of the street. "Is he like a hermit and super depressed?"

"Well, after it happened, we didn't see much of him for about a year, but then when we did, he seemed to be okay. Well… maybe not exactly the same, but… I don't know. He's a nice guy."

Connor starts walking again.

Wow! How can he still be okay after losing his wife and child? I slowly trail behind Connor, shaking my head.

A dark blue Durango sits in the driveway, and I see a light on in the upstairs window.

Connor rings the doorbell, and within a few seconds, the door swings open, revealing a man wearing red basketball shorts, black tank top, and earbuds in his ears.

"Mr. Karigan!" Connor exclaims like they are related or something.

"Connor!" Mr. Karigan shouts with a big smile on his face. "Oh, sorry guys. I was listening to a podcast about serial killers."

I flash Connor a horrified look, suspecting that they are both insane and using this dorky act as a cover up.

Mr. Karigan must have seen the look on my face, because he turns his attention to me. "It's a psychology podcast that studies and explains the behaviors of various mental disorders."

Okay, good, just a dork.

"Hey, Mr. Karigan!" Connor chirps like a boy band fan.

"It's Brad. Come on, you know I don't like formalities like that. Come on in, come on in." He motions us in while stepping aside.

Connor goes first, and I follow. His house is relatively normal like his wife had decorated it and he left it that way. We follow him around the corner and into his office.

"Whoa!" I exclaim. Mr. Karigan turns, smiling.

His office is like something from one of those movies where bookshelves line entire walls from floor to ceiling, with a tall ladder attached. Almost every space is taken by books, new and old. An old music machine sits on one side, aligned with albums produced by people I've never heard of. Two fancy looking leather chairs rest side by side in front of a massive antique desk covered with Victorian carvings. A tall, studded wingback chair is pulled up to the desk. Pictures of Albert Einstein and Abraham Lincoln frame each side of the room. An easel nestled in the corner is all marked up with handwritten notes. My eye catches the corner of the flip chart paper where red handwriting had been scrawled: 'Face the enemy!' I can't help but wonder who his enemy is. Strolling over to his desk chair, he plops down and motions for us to sit in the tall leather chairs. Sitting down, I notice all the candles around the room. These aren't the candles Mom burns that declare 'apple pie,' but instead majestic ones, as if they came from *Phantom of the Opera* or someplace like that.

Mr. Karigan walks over and lifts the lid of his music machine to place a large disc on top.

"What is that?" I ask.

He sets a long arm with a needle down on the disc and old-time music starts playing. "A record player. Ha! I guess I really am getting old. Actually, these were around long before my time, but I love old things," he says, smiling and adjusting the nobs. Once he is content with the sound of the record player, he turns to Connor. "Who is this?"

"Beethoven, right?"

Mr. Karigan raises his eyebrows in surprise.

"Hate to break it to you, but Beethoven died nearly 200 years ago." Mr. Karigan looks at me and then back at Connor.

"Oh! You mean… Haha! I thought you meant the music. Yes! This is—"

"Lawson Peters," I reply, cutting Connor off. I don't know whether to stand and introduce myself or not, because these leather chairs make me feel like I am in the Oval Office. "I'm… new. We moved into the brown—dark brown—house up there." I point and then quickly change direction, realizing that I have no idea where my house sits from here.

"Ohh, yes, yes," he pipes in. Living in the subdivision for many years, Mr. Karigan must have known all the people and who had moved in and out. "The Bates used to live there. They had two little kids who were, well, rambunctious. Good people, though."

"That explains the scuff marks in my room."

Mr. Karigan laughs. "So, you're in Connor's grade?"

"Yeah."

"Connor is a good kid. He cuts my grass every week. And, no, this is not Beethoven. Close. It's another German composer, Mendelssohn."

"Yeah, about the grass," Connor jumps in. "I'm going out of town tomorrow morning, so I wanted to see if you're okay with Lawson cutting your grass."

Mr. Karigan studies me as if examining whether or not I am capable to cut his grass.

"Can you cut grass?"

"Uh, yeah. I used to cut our yard at our old house."

"Hmm. At what level should one cut the grass this time of year?" he asks with his chin up in the air, like a grass scholar.

"One should cut it… short."

Mr. Karigan looks at Connor.

Connor smiles. "One should cut it tall, because it's hot and the tall grass provides more shade for keeping the dirt from getting too dry."

"Geez, you are brilliant, Mr. Brandt!" Mr. Karigan exclaims, pointing a finger at Connor and then making a touchdown sign in the air.

Mr. Karigan settles back into his previous expression and looks at me again.

"Okay, cut it tall," I respond, semi-amused by their little act.

"How much of the grass should you cut at any particular time?"

I stare at Connor.

"Never more than one third of its length," Connor boasts.

I slowly lift my arms like a touchdown but then realize I am not sure if that is the correct answer, and so I quickly put my arms back down.

Looking at Mr. Karigan and with a little hesitation I say, "Never more than one-third of its length."

Mr. Karigan stands up and reaches his hand out. "You're hired, Mr. Peters."

I shake his extended hand as he looks me straight in the eye. He has a confidence about him that seems genuine, but obviously he doesn't take himself too seriously. I'm not used to looking people in the eye like that, but for some reason, he makes it okay.

"Let me now show you my mean-green cutting machine, Lawson."

We walk into his garage, and I expect to see some top-of-the-line mower. Instead, in the corner of the room sits an old, walk-behind mower with grass stains all along the sides.

Noticing the disappointment on my face, he says, "What? You were expecting a John Deer rider?"

"No, it's good," I reply quickly.

"It's old, but you're right. It's good."

He kneels beside the weathered mower. "Usefulness beats appearance," he says. "People judge things and other people by their appearances, as if that determines value, but value is determined by what you get out of something after what you put into it over a period of time."

I nod, pretending I knew what any of that meant.

He could tell I didn't.

"What's the purpose of a lawn mower?" he asks us.

"To cut grass!" Connor shouts like a private in the army.

"Connor, seriously, man, let Lawson get the easy ones."

"To cut grass," I reply.

"And, to cut grass, what do you need?"

"A lawnmower." I reply.

"A broken lawnmower?" Mr. Karigan asks.

"No, of course not. One that works."

"Hmm," he says. "One that works with a dull blade?"

"With a sharp blade."

"One that works with a sharp blade, old oil, and a dirty air filter?"

"No. One with clean oil filter," I correct him confidently.

"One that works with a sharp blade, clean oil, clean filter, and a shiny exterior?"

"No."

"No, what?"

"You don't need a shiny exterior, but a rider would be better because you could cut more."

"Ahh, Mr. Lawson. You're a man who thinks after all. So, you're talking about efficiency on top of effectiveness, cutting it faster without sacrificing quality."

"That's right, and I prefer Lawson instead of the formalities," I say, smirking.

He glances over at a grinning Connor and then back at

me. "Well, Lawson. I think a walk-behind is better than a rider."

"Why? Don't you like efficiency?"

"I love efficiency. But you see, I like to think while I cut grass, and a walk-behind allows me to do just that."

"Can't you use the time you save with a rider to think inside?"

Mr. Karigan laughs while clapping his hands as if applauding me. "You're right! But, I like to walk while I think. Plus, I like to get exercise by cutting the grass. So, you see, for me a walk-behind is very efficient. This is what you call a paradox."

"A paradox?"

"Yeah, a paradox is something that seems to contradict itself but reveals a deeper truth through its contradiction. For example, less is more. So, in this case, by cutting grass I can work out, think, and get my grass cut all at the same time rather than doing all of those things separately. I actually save time not using a riding mower."

I stand in silence for a few seconds, trying to keep up with his logic.

"Besides," he exclaims, "there's a big hill in the back that a rider can't go on... so... yeah."

"So, we talked about all of that for no reason?" I ask.

"Not very efficient, are we?" Mr. Karigan laughs heartily while opening the garage door.

"You can cut anytime tomorrow morning, Lawson. Just come by and ring the doorbell."

"Okay! I will." Stepping back into the blinding sun, I realize that I had forgotten to thank him. "Oh, and Mr. Karig—" I catch myself after remembering he likes to be called by his first name, but I couldn't think of it. "Mr.—"

"Brad," he corrects me while checking the oil in the mower.

"Yeah, Brad. Thanks for the opportunity," I say quickly, feeling that Brad just might be my silver lining in this neighborhood.

"There will be more to come," he replies before turning back into his house.

Connor and I start walking back toward the pool. Thinking about what Mr. Karigan said, 'more to come,' I nudge Connor. "What did he mean by 'more to come?'"

Connor is messing with the tag on his t-shirt. "Oh, Brad is always having me think about stuff that usually ends in assignments."

"Assignments?"

"Yeah, like, well… I don't know."

Connor got quiet as if he decided midsentence that he didn't want to tell me.

"Like what?"

"Well, I told him that I struggle with, with being shy, so he wants me to talk to more people." Connor looks down at the ground and then at the pool.

"Ohh, that's why you're at the pool so much! That's why you talked to me!" I finally piece everything together.

He smiles, feeling relieved, knowing that I am still okay with him. "Yeah, that's why."

Suddenly, I find myself feeling differently about Connor, almost guilty, like I had been judging him. Yeah, exactly like I was judging him.

"Well, I'm glad you did," I say, smiling and hardly believing the words that came out of my mouth.

Connor lights up like a Christmas tree, and I could tell that he wants to say something, but he keeps it in.

We approach the intersection at his house before the road turns toward my house.

"Okay, Lawson, well, nice meeting you, and, I guess, I'll see you when I get back."

His awkward facial expression reminds me of a little boy talking to Santa Claus. "Nice meeting you too, Connor. Have a good trip, and I'll see you when you get back." I wave at him as he walks away and actually feel emotion toward him, like a pet turtle I was taking care of. For a moment I wonder if maybe I can work on him and actually make him cool... nah.

Walking back to my house, I think about Brad. He seems like a cool guy but not the cool I am used to; smart but not too dorky. He is nice but also confident. He is thirty-five, but he doesn't seem like a weird adult.

Walking through the front door, I am enveloped with paint fumes. I look up to see Mom painting the spindles.

"Hey, sweetie. Did you have a good time at the pool? Oh, shoot!" she says, grabbing a rag to wipe a drop of paint off the carpet.

"Yeah, I actually did, believe it or not. I met two new friends." Walking into the kitchen, I hear her footsteps coming down the stairs. I turn around to see her brush still in her hand with her eyebrows arched in a 'tell me more' look.

I grab a glass from the cabinet. "Yeah, a kid my age named Connor and a neighbor guy named Brad."

"Well, this is super, sweetie!" Mom grins happily, probably thinking that our family isn't falling apart after all.

"Brad wants me to cut his grass tomorrow for $40," I say, grabbing the O.J. from the fridge.

I thought Mom was literally going to pull out a Champaign bottle. "Doug! Are you hearing this?"

"What?" Dad yells from upstairs.

"Lawson is cutting a neighbor's yard tomorrow for $40!" she yells back up.

Dad runs down the stairs, wearing his old paint shirt and shorts. "Dude! Lawson! That's my boy being ambitious!" He comes over with his hand in the air for a high-five. I don't leave him hanging.

My parents hover over me like I just got accepted into Harvard.

"Yeah, yeah, yeah. Okay. You guys can go back to painting or whatever now."

Mom does a little dance up the stairs with her brush high in the air, and Dad trails behind, talking the entire time as he follows. "See, I told you, Linda. Everything is going to work out fine. And once we get these spindles done, then I…"

I chuckle to myself as I down the last of my juice.

Maybe this will all work out after all.

Maybe.

CHAPTER 3

I wake up to the sound of a train in the distance.

10 a.m.

I love sleeping in. Some people say that teenagers are lazy for sleeping so much, but I read somewhere that it's a proven fact that teenagers need more sleep. Our bodies are growing and our minds our developing—or something like that.

Grass! I'm cutting Brad's grass today!

I run downstairs to the refrigerator and pull out a frozen breakfast burrito. Thank goodness for microwaves. How did people even live without them? Dad is in the living room reading.

"Hey, Dad. Where's Mom?"

Dad lays down his book. "She's not feeling well today."

We know what that means when Mom isn't 'feeling well;' it doesn't mean she has the flu. It means that she is struggling with her anxiety and depression.

"Man, I wish she didn't have that. Is she taking her medication?"

"Yeah, but apparently it's not working, and you know about the side effects," Dad answers, frustrated.

Mom has been having nausea and even some insomnia lately from her 'sad pills,' as I call them. She says it all started in her twenties and then went away for a while but then came back about five years ago. She is forty-three now. I never really understood it, because one day she would be doing pretty good, but the next day she would barely come out of her room. I would ask her if she wanted to take a walk or go hang out with one of her friends, but she would tell me that she doesn't feel like it. 'That's why you need to get out,' I would tell her, but she would sigh and respond that I don't understand. I guess I don't.

Mom used to work at the school as a lunch lady, and she drove a bus, but she hasn't found a new job here, yet. She's hoping to get hired at my new school district. She was always cool about it, working at my school. She kept a low profile around me, which was kind of her style anyway. I would say that she is the introvert of the family, even though she is more of the talker at home. You know, like, she can't handle too many people at once, especially strangers. She gets drained in social settings and needs some quiet time to recharge. Dad and I are kind of opposite from her. I would say that we're more extroverts. We're not afraid to talk to strangers and we actually get energized from socializing even though we don't often talk to each other.

I take my plate to the sink and pop a multivitamin. "Well, I'm going to cut grass for Brad."

"Oh, yes, good! Hey, what is Brad's last name?"

I chuckle, thinking about the formalities thing but decide to let Dad figure it out on his own. "Karigan."

"Mr. Karigan. Okay, you'll have to introduce me sometime."

"Okay, Dad. See ya."

Even though the clouds cover the sun, it's already warming up. There is this beautiful thing in the state of Missouri called humidity. It's like living in an armpit for two months. The only good thing to do after 10 a.m. is to swim.

Brad's blue Durango is in his driveway, so I ring his doorbell. I take a step back, expecting the door to fling open with Brad standing there and his earbuds in, but nothing happens. I wait 15 seconds.

Do I ring the bell again? My mind starts racing. *Did he change his mind? Is he sick? Is he dead?* My finger reaches for the bell when the door finally opens.

"Lawson! Sorry, I was cleaning dishes. Why don't you get to cutting, and let me know when you're done. I'll open the garage door."

"Okay!" He seems to be in a good mood again today. How can he be so positive after losing his wife and child?

I walk around to the side of the house. The garage door is open, but Brad is not in sight. He must have pushed the button and went back inside. I walk over to the mower and see that it's already filled up and ready to go. I check the height settings and see that they look good—not too low. Our yard at our old house had never been pristine like the houses around here, probably because we didn't have a sprinkler system. I never minded cutting grass, though. Brad is right. It is a good way to think and get exercise.

I pull the choke on the side and then pull the cord. It starts right up. Maybe I should see if I can cut some other neighbors' yards. I could use some more money. My parents are pretty strict about me spending my own money. I think it's mostly Dad trying to teach me "the importance of a dollar," as he says. They're good on my birthday and Christmas, though. I heard that some people are more into giving and getting gifts than others; well, that's my parents. They love surprises and surprising others.

As I round the corner with the mower, I see Connor's house with no cars in the driveway. He must be on his way to church camp. My family never went to church, but that doesn't mean I'm against it. I just haven't thought about it much, I guess. The whole God thing confuses me. My aunt and uncle go, and they tell me that we all have a purpose in this life, because we were created, and all creations have a purpose—not sure what my purpose is. For now, at least, my purpose is to cut grass.

I'm almost finished with the front yard. My nose is full of that fresh cut grass smell—possibly the best scent in the world. It reminds me of football. Suddenly, an anxious feeling grows inside me. Football starts soon, and I don't know any of the players. I played quarterback at my old school, but we weren't that good. The front line was kind of weak, so I got sacked all the time. Part of me kind of likes the idea of a challenge to see if I can be the best player here. But part of me doesn't. Oh yeah, and my new coaches! Maybe they will be super strict like army drill sergeants. I always hated that type of personality, because I don't respond well to yelling. Never have. I don't curl up and oblige. I want to yell back.

Moving toward the backyard, sure enough, there is a hill. Brad was right. This wouldn't be good for a riding lawn mower. The backyard has two oak trees at each corner of the fence line and a small garden in between. My mind drifts back to the upcoming year. There is so much time. Four years. Four years to make new friends. Four years to go to state. Four years to not be an adult. What would my life have been like if I had stayed in my old home? Dad says that I would just be a big fish in a small pond, which I think means that even though I'm popular and good at sports there, it doesn't matter, because it is a small town. Anyone can do it. The true test is, can you do it in the city with real competition? Honestly, part of me agrees. I've always been competitive. Some people hate pushing themselves. Me? I get a thrill out of it. I would like to play football in college. I also want to have a good life and not be some loser who can't pay his bills. I don't know, though. I miss my friends.

I miss everything that was familiar, everything that was safe. I miss Emory. Seriously, though, the next four years could suck. Four years of no friends and being stuck with Connor. Four years of not playing sports, because I was cut from the team, or worse, forced to sit on the bench. I wipe the beaded sweat forming on my forehead. Is it scorching, or am I just having a minor anxiety attack or one of those minor hot flashes that Grandma used to have? No, wait, those have to do with estrogen or something.

All done. That wasn't too bad. I could do this every week. Maybe Brad will like me more, and he will fire Connor. That's mean, but still.

Brad opens the door and, sure enough, has his ear buds back in. But, he's more dressed up today, wearing blue khaki shorts and a white button-up polo shirt.

"Good! You didn't steal my mower. You never know about new teenagers who move in. Juice or Gatorade?" he asks, motioning me inside and walking toward the kitchen.

"Juice. Thanks." Not sure what is appropriate at Brad's house, I stop and take my shoes off, even though we didn't do it yesterday and I never did it at friends' houses in my old town.

He comes right back with my glass of orange juice and a glass of some weird apple looking juice for himself.

"Let's go into my office, man."

I'm not used to adults calling me 'man.' It usually sounds

way too fake or like they haven't accepted their oldness yet. Brad, for some reason, though, can get away with it. Kind of like when someone has a British accent and they seem smarter and cooler than everyone else no matter what they say.

"You know, I was spying on you—not like some creepy stranger—but checking over your work, and you did a pretty good job, Lawson." Brad sits down in his office chair and makes himself comfortable.

"Thanks."

Brad takes a sip of his drink and looks out the window.

"What is that?" I ask.

He looks behind himself. "What is what?"

"That drink," I say, pointing to his glass.

"Oh, Kombucha!" He takes another swig and sets it down.

"I never heard of it."

"Really? Well, not everyone drinks it. It's fermented tea. I brew my own. It's much better that way. You can also make different flavors. This one is ginger, and it is carbonated from the fermenting. Also, it's a probiotic, so it's good for your stomach," he says, holding the glass in the light as if examining it like a master brewer.

"So, it's alcoholic?"

He looks at me surprised. "No! Although it's possible to make it alcoholic if you brew it long enough. Boy, am I glad you asked. I wouldn't want you to go home and say that you were drinking with the neighbor guy!"

"Hey," he says after taking another sip, "I don't know much about you; so, tell me, where did you move from?"

"We moved from a small town in the middle of Missouri, and… uhh…"

"And you didn't want to move."

I nod. "You got it. My dad is forcing my life to be what he wants it to be."

"Why does he want to do that?"

I shrug. "I don't know—probably because he doesn't want me to fail at life, and he thinks that a small town doesn't have enough opportunity for me."

Brad stands and walks toward his bookshelf.

"I know what you're talking about, Lawson. He wants the best for you, but you feel like he doesn't care about what you want for your own life."

"That's right."

"But, I don't think he's afraid you will fail him so much as he is afraid that he will fail you."

"What?"

"What's your grandpa like?"

"He's is basically a mountain man who lives in a shack."

"Does he have a beard?"

"Yes!"

Brad laughs. "This guy sounds awesome. Now, this is just a hunch, but I have read a lot of psychology stuff, and I have some of my own personal history to pull from. It seems that even though your dad probably loves your grandpa, he was embarrassed as a kid living like that. So, he decided to get an education so that he could make enough money and give his family a lifestyle that he never had."

"Wow, that actually makes a lot of sense."

"So, your father is more concerned about not failing you than about you failing him." Brad says looking at his bookshelf.

Reaching up, Brad pulls a green book off the shelf. "What do you like?"

"What do I like?"

"Yeah."

"Well, I like football. I was the starting eighth grade quarterback, and I want to start as a JV quarterback this year."

"Cool. I look forward to seeing you play. You know, sports are funny. Like, our culture is obsessed with them, right?"

I nod my head.

"Well, let me ask you. Why do you love football so much?"

I don't even know how to answer that question. It's like asking why I love air or food so much.

"I don't know. I've always loved football. It's fun."

"Would it be fun if you played, but no one kept score?" Brad asks while seeming to know something I don't.

"I don't know. I mean, no, not as much. It's fun to win."

Brad pauses and then decides to change the conversation.

"Do you have a girlfriend?" Brad asks while sitting down with the book still in his hands.

My mood shifts by his question. "Yeah. But, not really. Her name is Emory, and we've been together for nine months, but I moved, so…"

"And, you love her?"

"Yes."

"Does she love you as much?"

"Yes, and probably more."

"And you don't want to break up with her?"

"No."

"But you feel like you might have to because of this move?"

"Yeah."

"Do you wish that she would break up with you instead?"

I never thought of that. Just the idea of Emory breaking up with me sounds terrible. "I don't know," I say, looking at the floor.

Brad lays the book on the desk and leans back in his chair with his arms folded. "I bet she is thinking all the same things. Sounds like you have a paradox, Lawson."

I kind of remembered that word from the lawn mower discussion yesterday. "Something making sense, but not really, right?"

"A paradox is something that seems to contradict itself but reveals a deeper truth through its contradiction. For example,

'We, as a culture, have more money and opportunities but less contentment. We have more ways to communicate with cell phones and computers but less meaningful communication.' These are paradoxes. Anyway, enough about that for now. Tell me, what else do you like?"

"Um, I like Chinese food."

"Haha, good, because if you don't like Chinese food, I don't think we can be friends anymore." Brad looks down at the green book. "Do you like to read?"

"Ehh," I wasn't sure what to say because I didn't want to let the man with wall-to-wall bookshelves down. "Kind of."

"So, I'll take that as a no." He smiles and then shrugs. "Well, it's probably because you haven't read any good books."

He plops down the old green book.

"*The Giving Tree*? Ha! I loved that book. Wait, you want me to read this?"

"Yes."

"Oh, okay, but I read this when I was like three years old."

"But this time I want you to find the paradox in it, and I think you'll find your answers to your dad and girlfriend. Remember, a paradox seems to contradict itself but reveals a deeper truth through its contradiction. Oh, and then there are also things called oxymorons, which are like two-word paradoxes. 'Jumbo shrimp' and 'bittersweet' are both examples. Shrimp are tiny, so calling them jumbo is a contradiction. It's an oxymoron. Plus, how can something be bitter and sweet at the same time? Well, we both know it can."

I lift the book and look at the cover. It shows a boy reaching up to the apple hanging off the tree.

"Come see me tomorrow and let me know what you found out," Brad says, reaching into his drawer. "Here is your $40. Good work today. Thanks again for covering for Connor."

We walk toward his front door, and I notice his flip chart again and point to it. "Oh, hey, what does 'face the enemy' mean?"

Brad pauses and then smiles as he opens the door. "We better save that for another day. See you tomorrow, bud."

"Oh, okay. See ya," I reply, stepping outside.

I feel kind of bad for asking him that. It's none of my business, but I can't help but wonder. Is he in trouble? Who is his enemy? Looking down at the book, I wonder what paradox he's talking about and if I even truly understand what a paradox means. Brad said that a paradox is something that seems to contradict itself but reveals a deeper truth through its contradiction. Hmm... I'm not sure. Who is his enemy? It's really bugging me...

Dad is messing with something under his gray truck hood and notices me walking up. Slamming it shut, he smiles and says, "There's my entrepreneur. How did it go?"

I wave the two twenties in the air.

"Fantastic! It went good?"

"Piece of cake. And he even gave me a book to read," I say, holding up *The Giving Tree.*

"What? That's a kid's book."

"Yeah, but he said there's a deeper meaning."

"Huh. Well, he seems like a nice guy. Hey, I'm heading to Walmart. Do you want to come and drive by your new school?"

Going back to the pool without Connor was my original plan, but a glimmer of hope flashes over Dad's eyes as he waits for my response. I think of what Brad said about my dad not wanting to fail me.

"Sure, why not," I say, opening the truck door and climbing in.

Dad turns on the engine, and the radio comes on blasting 80's music. "Come on, feel the noise. Girls, rock your boys. We'll get wild, wild, wild—"

Dad turns it down quickly. "Geez! Sorry about that."

"Hahaha! That's awesome," I say, laughing.

"I thought you didn't like 80's music?"

"I don't! I just think it's hilarious. You must have been rocking out the last time you were driving to get milk or something, huh?"

Dad laughs. "Yup, you got it."

Dad starts singing along to the song.

"Whoa! Whoa, Dad, who sings this song?"

"Quiet Riot—"

"Well, let's keep it that way," I say, smiling.

"Good one," Dad smirks. "I walked right into that joke."

I stare out the window at the houses passing.

"Wait! Quiet… what?"

"You already got me, dude. I'm not saying it again."

"No, I'm serious this time. Quiet what?"

"Quiet Riot."

"Is that a paradox?"

Dad leans his elbow against the side window pane and puts his finger to his chin. "Huh. Yeah, or like an oxymoron, I guess."

"Oh yeah, oxymoron, which is like a two-word paradox, right?"

"Right. How did you know that?"

"Brad taught me today."

"Well, looks like you have a free tutor for school. Fantastic!"

I see the strip mall on my right that Dad was talking about.

"Hey, Dad. Check out that Chinese restaurant." In large glowing letters, 'East China' seemed to glow on the brick building.

I absolutely love Chinese food. General Tso's is my favorite. A little kick of spice mixed with a touch of sweetness or something. I don't know. It's just amazing.

"Oh, yeah! We should pick up some for lunch and take it back to Mom," Dad says, still tapping on his steering wheel to his music.

Next to East China is what looks like a coffee shop.

"Hey, Dad, can you drop me off at that coffee shop over there, so I can read my book?"

"Sure, and I'll pick you up when I get done buying groceries. You can also place our Chinese orders for us."

Dad pulls into the parking lot and lets me out.

"See ya!" he shouts, driving away.

The sign reads, "Pat's Coffee," along with a picture of a hot steaming cup of coffee right next to it.

Ding dong; the door chimes as I walk inside. I hate how doors do that, because it always attracts everyone's attention to you. I give a little nod to the table of elderly people staring at me. Walking up to the counter, I see a big menu on a huge chalkboard on the back wall. To the left of the counter are two brunette-haired teenage girls making some kind of a drink. I figured this would be like an old man coffee shop serving two types of coffee: black or black. Actually, it's kind of cool. There are couches and chairs strategically placed around a fireplace with books on a table and abstract paintings on the walls.

"Can I help you?" the barista asks me, jarring my attention back to my order.

"Oh, yeah, a medium cappuccino, please," I reach inside

my pocket and grab my wallet.

"$3.53," she happily informs me from under her "Pat's Coffee" hat.

I hand her a $5 bill.

"Here's your change. It will be ready over there on that counter in just a couple of minutes." She gives me a quick smile and then directs her attention to the lady standing behind me.

"Okay, thanks." While waiting, I start walking toward a wall where several abstract paintings are displayed. Why do people like these things? Anyone can do this. Heck, a dog can do this. Just let him roll around in some paint and have a canvas ready when he shakes it off. I don't know. Maybe I just don't get this type of art.

An elderly group of men are in the center of the room talking about stuff. "Yeah, he worked on Tanner Boulevard. Good ole' Gary. He and I would go…"

I block out their conversation, because when you are forced into overhearing another person's conversation that you have absolutely no idea what that person is talking about, you want to throw something.

I wonder who painted all these canvases. It must have taken a long time. This one is not bad, actually. Colors of green, yellow, and white swirl in circles like waves—

"You can sit if you want."

"What?" I realize that I had reached the end of the room.

Sitting in a beanbag in a corner five feet away is a long blonde-haired girl with her legs crossed, and she is peaking over her book, looking at me.

"Oh, didn't see you there. Sorry. Um, I'm waiting on my coffee, but thanks," I stammer, embarrassed of my mindless wondering.

"Okay," she replies, pulling the book back over her eyes.

I turn and walk back to the counter.

She's pretty.

She is very pretty.

"Here's your cappuccino." The barista sets the coffee down and quickly goes back to mixing another drink.

"Thanks." I grab the cappuccino but then pause, not knowing where to go. Why do I feel this way? Does that girl like me? Is that why she asked me to sit, or is she just being nice, and I was rude by declining? I take a sip of the froth and pretend to be looking at one of the abstract paintings that I don't care about.

I have a girlfriend. I mean, I don't know. Am I allowed to talk to girls? It doesn't mean I am going to ask her out or anything. This is weird. I glance over, and the book is still covering her face. She's wearing a bright yellow dress with white dots and brown sandals.

I want to talk to her.

I walk over with my cappuccino and sit down in the chair across from her. She peaks over her book again, and I can tell by her eyes that she's smiling without seeing her mouth. She lifts it back over her eyes.

What should I say? Just play it cool. Don't be weird. You're just sitting here, enjoying a cup of coffee. Not wanting to seem strange, I pick up my book—oh great, real cool. What 14-year-old guy reads *The Giving Tree* at a coffee shop? I lay it down on my lap so she doesn't see the cover.

Once there was a tree... and she loved a little boy. I flip the page and get a flashback of sitting on Mom's lap when I was three. I always liked this book.

...and every day the boy would come, and he would gather her leaves and make them into crowns and play king of the forest.

"Is that *The Giving Tree*?"

I pop my head up and see the girl taking a sip of tea with her book on her lap.

"Oh, umm..." I reply, trying to figure out what to say.

"I saw it in your hands when you were looking at the painting," she says, grinning.

Without a good lie, I respond, "Yeah, my neighbor gave it to me today and told me to find the deeper meaning in it." I glance at the cover again.

"I love that book." She leans forward. "You've read it, right?"

"Yeah, a long time ago. It's kind of sad, actually. The boy takes everything from the tree until the tree is just a stump." I flip through some pages.

"Yeah, but the tree chose to give those things to the boy." She leans back, resting herself against the wall and smiles as if she just read it this morning and did a book report.

I think for a second. "Well, maybe you can help me find the deeper meaning. So, it's about not using people or things, right? Not taking their love for granted?"

"Too easy." She gets up, walks toward me, and sits down in the seat next to me. A wave of her perfume follows her and finds my nose. Soft. Her scent and her voice, and her smile... It's all so *soft.* "That's too obvious, so it can't be that." She gestures for the book and flips through the pages until she comes to the part where the boy is hugging the tree. She reads aloud, "*And the boy loved the tree.*" Glancing up at me, her eyes are ice blue and her blonde hair is completely straight. "So, the boy loved the tree."

"Yeah, but he took everything," I counter her. "The leaves, apples, limbs, and even the trunk. He didn't give anything back to the tree."

"He gave his company," she adds. "Besides, the tree didn't want anything. It just wanted him to be happy."

I grab the book from her hands and flip toward the middle. "*But, the boy stayed away for a long time... and the tree was sad.*' See, the boy didn't even spend time with the tree when it got older and that made the tree sad."

She leans back with her head tilted in thought. "I think the tree understood. It knew the boy didn't understand love."

I smile, leaning back in my chair also. "Okay, so what is… love?"

Clearing her throat, she sits up straight as if answering a spelling B question.

"Love is giving without needing to receive," she says confidently.

"But, that obviously made the tree sad."

She grabs the book back and flips to the end. "*The old man was sitting on the trunk… 'I am very tired.' 'Well,' said the tree straightening herself as much as she could. 'An old stump is good for sitting and resting. Come boy, sit down. Sit down and rest.' And the boy did. And the tree was happy.*"

"So, the tree was happy and sad at the same time?" I ask.

"Kind of. I prefer the phrase 'bittersweet,'" she says, looking at the ceiling.

"Bittersweet?"

"Yeah, like something can be happy and sad at the same time."

"Wait." I start laughing.

"What?"

"Has everyone been using oxymorons this entire time and I am just now noticing, or is this something new?"

"Haha. What?"

"My neighbor, the guy who is making me read this again, was talking to me about paradoxes and oxymorons. Bittersweet; it's an oxymoron. You know, like a two-word paradox."

"Yeah, I guess that makes love an oxymoron." She laughs and hands me the book.

"Still, though, what's the deeper point?" I ask desperately.

"Well, okay, so, love needs to give, because that's what it's made for, right?"

"Okay."

"And, even though it has to give up things to love some-one, it's worth it."

"Why is it worth it?"

"Because."

"I mean, what if that boy never came back? Would it still have been worth it?"

She sat thinking for a second, looking for the right words.

"I guess the tree wasn't expecting something in return," she replies, looking straight ahead, trying to figure it out. "Besides, even when almost every physical part of the tree was gone, the tree's love was just as big as it was when it started. Actually, it seems like it has even more love for the boy as time goes on."

"Yes, yes, yes! We're getting it. You learn to love… when… you learn to… let go."

She put up both hands over her heart, as if she finally found it. "The more love you give, the more love you have."

"Sounds like a paradox," I say, smiling.

She starts clapping and bouncing in her chair but then stops when she attracts the attention of the senior citizen table.

"Thank you. Wow. Seriously, you... you are very smart."

"Nope," she says, sticking out her hand. "I'm Willow."

"I'm Lawson."

She has a soft grip, and her fingernails are painted light pink. I must have held on too long, because she slowly pulled her hand away.

"Um," I hesitate. "Do you go to Mill Valley?"

"Yeah, freshman. You?"

I literally let out a small giggle. "Yeah. I'm new."

"I thought so," she says, smiling.

My phone rings in my pocket. "Oh, I bet that's my dad." I pull it out...

Emory.

I just stare at the phone as if she somehow has been watching everything from a hidden camera like one of those cheaters shows.

"Aren't you going to answer it?" Willow asks.

"Um... he's probably outside. I'll just head out," I respond, grabbing my book and trying not to seem too awkward.

"But, hey, I'll look you up. What's your last name?"

"Harrison," she says, going back to her seat with her tea and book.

"Ok, oh, and what are you reading?"

"Oh, just some deep, meaningful book about love," she smiles and gives a snooty look.

"And to think that I almost asked those guys for advice." I nod my head to the old guys behind us, still bantering about Gary.

"Bye, Lawson." She crosses her legs and takes a sip of her tea.

"Bye." I rush outside and, of course, don't see my dad anywhere. I head to the Chinese restaurant while pulling my phone out. One new voicemail…

"Hey, Babe, it went to your voicemail. Not sure what you're doing, but I was just thinking about you, and I know we haven't talk in a while. But… I'm going to the pool, so… just call me… bye."

What am I supposed to tell her? Sorry, I ignored your call because I was talking to a new, hot girl in a coffee shop? Oh yeah, no big deal. We were just talking about love and stuff. Emory would probably hitchhike up here just to punch me in the face. Actually, she would probably just be really hurt and cry. I mean, I would be mad if I knew she was flirting with a guy she thought was cute.

I open the door to the restaurant and step inside. The smell fills my nose. Oh, my gosh! Amazing! If I had to sniff a candle every five minutes for the rest of my life, I would choose the 'Chinese Restaurant' candle. I look at the menu but can't focus. I like this girl. I'm not trying to be a jerk, but I can't help it. I really like this girl. Willow. I even like her name. Can I like two girls at the same time? Obviously, I can because I do, but I can't because that's called cheating. Really, she reminds me of Emory but seems a little more mature and, well, confident.

"Hello, welcome to East China. Ready to order?" The lady behind the register is Chinese and has a big, warm smile.

"Yeah… I'll take a General Tso's, beef and broccoli, cashew chicken, and one large egg drop soup."

Those are some of my favorite words in the English language, in that order.

I pay up and wait by the window. I need to call Emory. I'll just say I was ordering Chinese food. I mean, it's not too far from the truth.

The phone rings… second ring… third ring…fourth—

"Hello?"

"Hey, babe! Sorry I missed your call. I was ordering Chinese food. Are you at the pool?" I asked, trying to sound like I was not a complete liar.

"Yeah, just got here. It was just weird because you never send me to voicemail," she says, sounding suspicious.

"Yeah, sorry about that, but I can call you tonight."

"Can you talk now? I miss you."

"I know. I miss you too, but I have to get this food, and Dad is waiting for me. I'll call you tonight."

"Okay. Bye." She hangs up irritated.

Could she sense anything weird from me? I didn't do anything wrong. Then again, why am I so nervous? I like this girl. That's why. I feel like I'm already cheating. Why am I freaking out? Willow might not even like me like that, and what if I break up with Emory, and then Willow doesn't go out with me? Then, I'll have no one. Wow, that sounds insecure.

"Here's your food, Sir." The lady hands me a big bag full of Chinese heaven.

I see Dad pulling up in the parking lot. Perfect timing.

I walk to his truck, holding the bag of food like a newborn baby.

"Hey, bud!"

"Hey, Dad." I climb inside.

"Got your book read?"

"Yeah." I reply, hoping he doesn't by chance ask me if I met a hot girl with an amazing personality.

"Good." Putting the gear shift in reverse, he backs out of the parking spot. "Let's go home and eat!"

"There's your school!" Dad says, pointing out his window.

It looks huge compared to my old school—fairly new, too. The front of the school is lined with stone pillars and there's a big football stadium on the side.

"Wow," I say, partly excited and partly terrified.

"You'll do great, bud. I've always seen a lot of potential in you. You're going to do amazing things here. I bet you even shock yourself," Dad says, nodding his head and looking at the school.

It feels good knowing that Dad believes in me, and I know he means it.

"Remember," he says, looking at me, "you're only a freshman once. You never get a second chance to be a freshman."

"Yeah… you're right." I look out the window at the empty school parking lot.

Dad's words stuck with me. Time is a funny thing, because it's not a two-way street. It only goes one way—forward, and you can't stop it or slow it down. My eighth-grade year is over. I'll never get it back, and the same will happen with my freshman and sophomore year… and then the rest of high school. Though today, it seems like a long time from now.

For now, Chinese food smells really good.

CHAPTER 4

"Mom, we have Chinese!" I take the boxes of food out of the bag and place them on the kitchen island.

No response.

I look at Dad. "Is Mom here?"

"Yeah, she should be upstairs." Dad walks to the bottom of the staircase. "Honey! You up there?"

No response.

I remember that her car is in the driveway.

"I'll check," Dad says, walking up the stairs.

I can hear Dad upstairs calling for Mom. I get horrible thoughts that Mom slipped and fell on something and is lying dead on the bathroom floor or a burglar came in to steal her jewelry and shot her… Dad comes back downstairs.

"She's not up there."

I get a sick feeling inside telling me that something is wrong. What if she killed herself? She has been depressed lately. But, there's no way she would do that. She's not feeling that bad, right? Although, they say that when someone committed suicide, most often no one was suspecting it. I look at the knife block in the kitchen and see that one is missing. It's not on the counter.

I walk around the corner to peak downstairs and notice a light on.

"Mom?" I call out slowly, walking down the steps.

No response. I see something black lying on the floor next to the basement door. Is that what I think it is? I take a few more steps down. It's the handle of the knife. I stop, not sure if I want to find out if the other end of the knife is clean or if it has blood on it.

"Dad?" I nervously call out.

"She probably just walked over to meet the neighbors or something," he says with a muffled voice.

I can hear Dad upstairs messing with the boxes of Chinese food. I take two more steps down and listen for anything on the other end. Silence. Reaching out, I place my hand against the basement door and pause as if bracing myself to see Mom's lifeless corpse on the concrete floor. I swing the door open. No one. Looking down, the blade is clean.

"Linda!" Dad calls out from upstairs.

I run upstairs and see Mom walking into the kitchen.

"Hey, guys." Mom pulls off her pink gloves and turns on the faucet to wash her hands. "I was pulling weeds on the side of the house."

I let out a big sigh.

"Chinese!" she exclaims with excitement.

"Mom, why is there a knife downstairs?"

Dad stops eating and looks from me to her.

"Oh, I was cutting a box open with it and forgot to bring it back up."

I shake my head and walk over to the plates. I chuckle to myself, thinking how much I got worked up. I'm turning into a worrier like my mom. Mom grabs her Cashew Chicken, while Dad is halfway done with his Beef and Broccoli. I grab my General Tso's Chicken and a side of sweet and sour. That's my little twist: dunk the General's Chicken in the sweet and sour. It's a life changer. And oh yeah, you can't forget about the egg drop soup.

"Lawson saw his new school," Dad says, wiping his mouth.

"Yeah? What did you think honey?"

"Big. Intimidating. But... exciting," I say with a little smile.

Both my parents smile, nodding their heads.

"You'll do great, Lawson," Mom says almost convincingly.

I scarf the rest of my food down and take my plate to the sink. Emory always told me I was a fast eater. Emory! I have to call her. Wait. What do I tell her? Are we going to break up? We need to break up, right?

I need to talk to Brad. Would it be weird if I went over there right now?

"Mom, dad, I'm going to check out the pool."

"Ok, bud." Dad says.

"Ok, sweetie!" Mom says.

I walk out the door and then realize that I almost forgot *The Giving Tree*. I go back inside and grab the book off the table. As I get down to the pool, I see his Durango in the driveway. Does he have a real job? As I approach the door, it swings opens and out walks Brad.

"Hey, Lawson, what's up?"

"Did you see me coming?" I ask startled.

"No, I was going to the grocery store, but I have time. You want to talk?"

"Yeah... actually, I do."

"Well, come on in, man," he says, backing up and holding the door open.

We walk into his office and take our usual seats.

"You read the book already?"

"Yeah, I actually did."

"OK, so what did you find?"

"Well, we found... I mean, I found that—"

"We? You had help?" He looks at me suspiciously as if I cheated on my homework.

"Yeah. A girl at Pat's Coffee."

"Well, well, well." He settles back into his chair and crosses his arms. "You dog, you, using *The Giving Tree* to pick up girls. That's a first." He leans forward, resting his elbows on his desk. "Go on..."

"Well, that's actually, kind of, why I'm here. So, I just

ran into this girl, and her name is Willow. She is super nice, pretty, and… smart, really smart—"

"And, now you like her, but you feel guilty because you still have a girlfriend back home," he says, finishing my thoughts.

"*Yes*! Yes. She… I don't know… well, this is what we came up with. OK, so, the book is a paradox about love. Love is bittersweet. The tree had to sacrifice. Well, it didn't have to, it chose to, because love needs to give. It wants to give. Even if almost every physical part of the tree was gone, the tree's love wasn't used up. It actually grew. So, the more love you give away, the more love you have."

I look at Brad, waiting for a celebration or applause or something.

He looks at me puzzled. "Did you or Willow come up with this answer?"

"We both did… but yeah she helped… a lot."

"Are you sure this pretty teenage girl isn't actually a wise seventy-five-year-old grandma named Evelyn?"

"Ha! Yes, I'm sure. Why, who is Evelyn?"

"No one. I just made her up trying to make sense of this *brilliance*!" he exclaims, putting his hand out and yelling at the ceiling.

"But wait…" He stops and looks back at me. "What does this have to do with you and Emory?"

Brad rests his elbows on his desk and leans forward,

awaiting my answer.

A moment of thought passes.

"I need to love Emory and stay with her no matter what? I need to give love, and then I will have more love?"

"Hmm… perhaps, but your situations might be different."

"How?"

"There comes a point when it's more loving to let someone go than to hold on."

"What do you mean?"

"Is Emory hurting right now?"

"Yes."

"What does she want?"

"For me to move back, so we can be together."

"Is that possible?"

"No."

"Will you hurt her more by breaking up now or breaking up later?"

"Later," I say softly, suddenly realizing what Brad was saying.

Brad repeats, "So… there comes a point when it's more loving to let someone go than to hold on."

"Bittersweet," I say, looking at the ground.

"Bittersweet," Brad repeats.

I take in a deep breath and let it out.

Brad tilts his head. "What are you thinking?"

"The last thing Emory said to me in person was, 'There's

no point holding on to something you have to let go of.'"

"There's more truth to what she said than she probably knows. Besides," he says, folding his arms, "it sounds like you're already interested in this other girl."

"Well—"

"No, it's okay if you are. It might make it easier for you to let go of Emory. But, if you are talking to this new girl, you definitely need to let Emory go."

"But... how? How do I break up with her?"

"How would you want her to break up with you?"

I never thought of that. "I guess I would want her to tell me straight up, but—gently."

"Me too," Brad replies.

I give him a painful smile. Brad walks over to me.

"Let me know how it goes, man," Brad says, giving a firm pat on the shoulder as I stand and we walk toward the door.

"Oh, and Lawson?" Brad says as I open the door. "I'm going to need that book back."

"Thanks again," I say, handing him the book and stepping outside.

"Lawson..."

I look back.

"Remember that a man is measured not by how he accepts the good times but by how he handles the hard times. Be gentle but be real."

I nod in agreement as he closes the door.

I step down off the front porch but then hear the door open again. I turn back around, expecting him to say something profound.

"Grocery store! Almost forgot." He quickly walks past me and toward his vehicle.

Looking over his shoulder, "It's good for us to remember that one person's 'milk day' is another person's 'lemon day.' But, the sour makes the sweet even sweeter." He places one hand on the door handle. "Come see me tomorrow, bud. I'll be thinking of you and Emory."

Brad hops in his Durango and takes off.

I know what I have to do, but I don't want to do it.

How did this all happen? Nine months ago, I had asked a brown-haired, freckled face girl if I could be her boyfriend. We were always kind of friends, but something clicked in eighth grade. We started to see each other a little differently. Our friends kept gossiping in our ears that we should go out, but I think she was afraid it might ruin our friendship if we ever broke up. Finally, one day after school, we were shooting basketball together in my driveway. We were playing HORSE, and I was about to win. She had to make a free throw to stay in the game. Just as she was about to shoot I said, "If you miss this shot, you have to be my girlfriend."

She paused and then smiled without taking her eyes off the rim. She took a deep breath and then shot it three feet over the backboard. We both started laughing, and we knew things would never be the same between us. Of course, she said I didn't really beat her, because she let me win.

She played a big part in making me a better person. We figured we would go out all through high school... and now today is the day that I'm going to break up with her.

A lemon day.

"How was the pool?" Mom asks.

I go straight up to my room, not paying attention to her question. I shut the door and lay on my bed. This sucks. I don't want to be the bad guy. Why can't we just both say it at the same time so that no one is to blame? I look at her name in recent calls, trying to delay the inevitable.

Like Brad said, "Be gentle, but be real."

I push the call button.

My heart starts beating. Maybe I'm over reacting. I should hang up—

"Hello?" Emory's voice was weak. She's been crying.

"Hey," I say.

"What's up?"

"Um... how are you?"

"Sad. This is the worst summer ever," she replies.

I pause with the realization that I am about to make it much worse. Maybe today isn't a good day for this. I should wait until she is in a good mood—

"Do you think we should break up, Lawson?"

I freeze, not knowing how to respond.

"Hmm, your silence is deafening!"

"Emory…"

"Is it that easy for you? What, you've been away for just a few days, and you already want to break up?"

"No. I don't want to break up, but how are we going to do this? Are we going to talk on the phone for a year until we can drive? Even then, we will do a six-hour round-trip drive every time we want to see each other?

"Maybe! Maybe we do! Maybe we try instead of giving up after just A FEW DAYS!" she screams.

I take a breath.

"I don't want to let go, Emory, but I just feel like holding on will cause us even more pain than letting go."

She's silent.

"Did you meet someone new?" she asks softly.

Silence.

"You're a pig. Goodbye, Lawson."

"*Wait*! Wait. Just wait, please… Look, if I had it my way, I would never have moved. I would be sitting right next to you, right now, and we would never break up. We would stay together all through high school. We would go to every school dance together, and our parents would have a collection of our pictures in some cheesy old high school album."

She starts crying.

I continue. "We would both play varsity sports and cheer each other on. And then we would sit by each other at graduation and throw our hats up in the air, and—"

"But, we won't." Emory cuts me off. "None of that will happen now because you moved, and you like someone new."

"Wait, that's not fair—"

"Not fair?" she yells. "Being dumped by my biological parents and now by my boyfriend is what's not fair!"

"Emory—"

"Have a great time in high school, Lawson! Bye!"

And, that's it.

It's over.

I don't know how I feel. I want to call her again, take it all back, and make the long-distance thing work. No. This is the right thing to do. Right? I take a deep breath, trying to calm down and keep myself from crying.

It's no use. Tears roll down my cheeks as I lean back against my door...in my room...in my town.

Lemons.

Chapter 5

Willow Harrison. Her profile picture pops up of her looking at the sky. That's her. I do like her, but I still feel guilty about Emory. Should I message Willow? No. Girls don't like a guy who is desperate. Maybe I'll wait a few days. Besides, I'll look like a serial dater if I contact Willow right after breaking it off with Emory.

A sudden knock at the front door draws me out of my online stalking. Connor comes back home from church camp today. I bet that's him, and I can't believe I'm saying this, but I look forward to seeing someone who likes me.

"Hey, Lawson!"

My attention is immediately drawn to his red, sunburned nose and contrasting blue hat that says, "Camp Christ."

"Hey, Connor," I say, stepping outside.

"Hey, do you want to come with me down to the train tracks?"

"Train tracks?"

"Yeah, it's a cool spot away from the houses where I go to just sit and think."

"That, Connor, actually, sounds perfect right now. Let's go!" I grab my phone and flip flops.

Connor leads me down the street and through some

backyards into the woods.

"Is this where the seemingly meek neighborhood boy tortures and then murders his unsuspecting neighborhood friend?"

"Yes."

"Haha, good Connor! You do have a sense of humor after all!" I step over a fallen tree limb covered with moss.

Connor stops and waits for me to catch up. "It's just through this opening."

"Theden," I read out loud, looking at the weathered street sign. As we continue to step over more fallen tree limbs, we finally come to an old country road. To my left is an open field, and to my right, bordering some trees, are train tracks.

Connor continues his guided tour. "This is the old road that, at one time, was the main, if not only, road before all of the subdivisions were built. There are a few old houses remaining, but other than that, nothing else."

"And no one ever comes here?"

"Nope, it's kind of my secret spot."

"Aww, this is so cute. You're sharing your secret spot with me." I frolic ahead of him, leaping in the air.

"I'm going to bury you up here, just to the right." Connor says, laughing a little too hard at his own joke.

We approach the train tracks, and I see another small field. It's beautiful, like a lost world. It must have been a farmer's field at one time, but now just prairie grass and a tall elm tree right in the middle.

"Dang, this is cool." I say admiring the old tree.

"I told you so. Follow me." Connor walks over to the huge elm tree. "This is Ned."

"Ned?"

"Yeah, I named the tree Ned."

"That's kind of weird. Actually, it's really weird."

"Well, trees make good friends, especially this one. It's perfect for climbing up and wait 'til you see the view!"

"If you break out in song, I'm going to puke."

"Trees lift you higher," Connor starts singing off key.

Connor jumps up on the lowest branch. "Let's go!" he says, looking to the top.

"Honestly, I've never climbed a tree."

"Don't be a dork," he calls down.

"Coming from you, Connor, that's really funny." I yell up as he is already on his way to the top.

Slowly and methodically, I make my way to the top. Connor is already sitting on a large branch and looking out onto the open field.

"Wow!" I can see the entire subdivision and even the school in the distance! "Did you trim some of these branches to get this view?"

"Yeah, a little, just to see better, but it shouldn't hurt the tree too much."

We look out at the picture-perfect view.

"So, how did Brad's yard go?"

"I don't know how to say this, but I probably replaced you. Basically, you should apply to Pat's Coffee or something, since you'll be unemployed now. Sorry, man."

"Sure. What else happened while I was gone?"

"Well, I broke up with my girlfriend."

"Geez!" Connor gives me a shocked look. "How did she take it?"

"Bad. I didn't enjoy it. I won't lie, I even cried a little."

"I would too if I had to break up with a girlfriend. Shoot, I'd cry if a girl asked me out."

"Hahaha, you actually seem secure in yourself, Connor," I say, looking at his peeling nose.

"Really? Well, I don't know. I've just learned to accept things and not have too high of expectations. I used to be really shy, but I've been working on that lately."

"But, doesn't Brad put high expectations on you?"

"Yeah. Well, he's always asking me what I want."

"He asked me that, too."

"Yeah? What did you say?"

"I want to start JV quarterback as a freshman, but since this is a bigger school, I'm afraid I might not even make the team."

Connor pulls a leaf from a limb, nodding his head.

"What do you what?" I ask.

Connor smiles and looks around at the scenery. "This."

It is beautiful up here. I can see why he loves it. We look at the empty train track that stretches about a mile ahead and then rounds a corner out of view.

"Hey, I met a girl at Pat's Coffee!"

"For me?"

"Seriously, her name is Willow, and she seems really cool."

"I know Willow!" Connor says whipping his head at me.

"You do?"

"Yeah, but she doesn't like me like that. We're just friends. She lives on the other side of the school."

"So, is she single?"

"Yeah, I think so. She doesn't date much."

"What does she like to do?"

"Well, she's always reading. She's actually really smart, but she's nice too, not too cool, ya know?"

"Yeah... yeah, I do," I say, smiling and imagining her sitting next to me at the coffee shop. "I bet she would like Brad."

"You're right, she would!"

"Great! Then, we should all hang out with him, sometime... soon."

"Wait, are you using me to hook you up with, like, my only friend?"

"I'm your friend too!" I exclaim, smiling cheesy and putting my hand on my cheeks.

"I don't know..." Connor says, seriously concerned.

"We could all be one big happy group," I assure him.

Connor thinks for a second. "*Don't* be a jerk and ruin this, OK?" He points his finger at me.

"Okay, okay… I won't." I raise my hands up in defense. "So, call her!"

"Geez, you seriously are desperate. I don't have her number, but I can tweet her or something."

Connor pulls his phone out and starts typing a message.

"Ask her to come today."

He murmurs what he is typing under his breath. "… There. Sent."

She immediately responds. "Okay, I'll ride my bike over in about a half hour."

I throw my arms up in victory.

"Wow, that was easy," Connor says in disbelief.

"Let's go get ready!" I say, climbing down without him.

"We don't even know if Brad is home today," Connor says, catching up to me.

"Well, then, let's go and find out!"

We rush back to Brad's house and see his Durango. Connor knocks on the door, and within seconds Brad opens the door wearing pajamas. He's smiling, but something is off. There's a tired sadness behind it all. When he smiles bigger, it's like he's just forcing it into the background.

"Oh, I'm sorry. Were you sleeping?" Connor asks.

Brad looks down at his clothes. "Heck no, Connor, these

are my work clothes today. You can wear whatever you want when you work at home."

"Hey, is it okay if we introduce you to our friend, Willow? She will be here soon," Connor asks.

Brad looks at me and grins suspiciously. "Can I keep my PJ's on?"

We both laugh.

"OK, good. Then come on in while I clean up a bit for our lady guest."

We walk inside and see papers lying around his office.

"Hey Brad, I'm curious. What do you do for a living?"

"I'm a writer. I write novels."

"About what?" I ask.

"Mysteries. But, I throw in a bit of romance, humor, too." Brad says, cleaning up the room.

"Cool. Have you made a lot of money from it?"

"Ha! That's a good one. Well, actually, I had a book about six years ago that did pretty good, but then… well, I had some issues in my life that made writing kind of hard."

I remember what Connor told me about Brad losing his wife and kid about five years ago.

Ding, dong.

Connor and I both jump up at the same time to get the door. I let him go ahead of me, thinking that I should probably play it cool. I look back at Brad, who is shaking his head and grinning.

Connor opens the door. "Come in, Willow!"

Willow is wearing white shorts and a pink tank top. Her hair is up in a ponytail with glasses on her head and black flip flops on her feet.

"Hey, Connor!" Willow gives Connor a little hug before noticing me.

"Lawson! How did your book report go?" she teases me.

I look back at Brad and then at Willow. "Well, you'll have to ask my teacher."

Brad walks over and extends his hand. "Pleasure to meet you, Willow. I'm Brad."

Willow shakes his hand. "I'm sorry that you are stuck with these two guys, Willow."

"God does have a sense of humor, doesn't he? Take a seat, everyone. Oh, I forgot! Wait here." Brad quickly dashes into the kitchen, while everyone else settles into our chairs.

"How's your summer?" Connor asks Willow.

"It's actually going really good. Got to read a bunch of books and even met some... interesting people at the coffee shop," Willow says while putting her hand up to block her voice, pretending as if I couldn't hear her.

"You really should stop harassing those old people," I say lounging back in my chair, trying to look like I don't have a big crush on her.

"OK, Grandma Brad is back with some Kombucha!" Brad holds up a big bottle and four plastic cups.

"You like Kombucha?" Willow perks up.

"Just a bit. Do you?"

"Yes!"

"This girl is definitely out of your league, guys," Brad confirms.

We both nod our heads.

"This is Mango Kombucha." He pours the orange, bubbly liquid into each cup of ice. "Give it a try."

"Mmm," Connor says.

"You should seriously sell this stuff," Willow says, smacking her lips.

I join in. "Not bad at all. Bubbly."

"You are all correct." Brad takes another swig and sets his cup down on his desk. "So, Willow," Brad says, taking his usual place behind his desk. "What do you want?"

"What do you mean?" she asks inquisitively while crossing her legs.

"What's the one thing, above all else, that you want?"

Willow squints her eyes, as she looks up at the ceiling, "Umm, I want... hmm... I want..."

"What do you *really* want?" Brad repeats.

"I really want... Okay, so this is what I really want, and I know it sounds cheesy, but I want people to be less fake. I want them to be real and not care about what others think so much. Usually, everyone in school cares about really stupid things, and they can be really mean. I want, I don't know, people to have more love." Willow starts laughing. "Sorry, I know that sounds like a Miss America pageant answer."

Brad shakes his head, chuckling. "Willow, I know it's impossible, but I think you're my twin sister."

"Yeah," I add, "Willow is probably a 35-year-old with some medical condition that makes her look 14. Seriously, Brad, she might know more than you."

Brad raises an eyebrow, sensing the challenge. "Okay, young lady. Let me ask you a question."

"Ask away!" Willow beams, sitting straight in her chair.

"What is the opposite of love?"

Willow tilts her head in thought. "The opposite of love is—hate."

Brad raises his eyebrows as if to say, "Are you sure?"

"Isn't it?" I butt in.

"Let me put it this way," Brad adds. "If I love animals, do I hate animal abuse?"

"Seriously, Brad, you're like a human Yoda," I say in disbelief.

Brad lets out a big laugh. "So, what's the opposite of love? And by love, I don't mean romance. Being in love is actually just infatuation. You 'love' that person, because you want them to 'love' you back. So, it's conditional, but we all know that true love is unconditional. You do what's best for someone, even if they don't do it back. That doesn't mean unconditional love doesn't feel good. It can feel great, but it can also hurt, because it requires sacrifice. All good things do. So, again, what is the opposite of love?"

No one had an answer.

"Well," Brad helps out, "to love is to care, so not to love is…"

"Not care!" I exclaim.

Brad points at me. "Boom. The opposite of love is indifference, apathy."

"Wow! Brad, you should teach at our school." Connor says.

Brad smiles. "I don't know about that, Connor."

"Or, maybe you can come to our school and speak," Willow adds.

"Speak?" I ask.

"Yeah, sometimes the school brings in motivational speakers to talk about drugs or whatever, and they're usually cheesy, but you, Brad, would be awesome!" Willow says enthusiastically.

"Hmm… that could be kind of fun, but I usually feel more comfortable behind a blank page with a pen in my hand… or with a few people who actually want to talk to me," Brad says, smiling at us. "Besides, they probably wouldn't let me wear pajamas. A toast to pajamas!" Brad raises his glass high in the air.

"To pajamas!" We all shout, raising our glasses.

How did I end up here? An endearing dork, a

30-something-year-old Yoda, an amazing girl, and me, a guy lost in his forsaken past and unknown future. It's like my life's file got mixed up with someone else's, and now I'm living his life, a different life, it seems, as I stare at the strangers in the room who somehow feel familiar. These three people make me feel accepted in a way I haven't felt before even though I was always popular. This kind of acceptance was a different kind, a simpler kind.

"Okay, everyone! Brad exclaims, setting his empty glass on the desk and standing up. "Time to get out. You might not think it, but I'm an important person with important things to do." Brad brushes off his pajamas as if they were a three-piece suit.

We thank Brad and head out.

Once outside, I notice Willow's bike in the driveway. "Aren't you a little old to be riding a bike?"

"Coming from 'The Giving Tree' guy?" she asks.

She had me on that one.

"Hey, Connor showed me a really cool spot off Theden road. Connor, let's take her there," I suggest.

"How generous of you to offer my not-so-secret-anymore spot, Lawson."

"Come on, it's too cool to be kept all to yourself!"

Connor looks at Willow and me and shrugs his shoulders. "Okay."

As we walk, Willow rides her bike around us while

chattering about why she's glad she's not in middle school anymore. My mind bounces between gawking at Willow and thinking about Brad's hidden sad face.

"Hey, did Brad seem sad today?" I ask everyone.

"Seemed fine to me," Connor replies.

"Yeah, he seemed happy," Willow adds.

"His wife and daughter died in a car accident five years ago." I say this, not knowing if Willow knows.

Willow abruptly stops her bike. Her eyes pop open in shock and then immediately soften with sadness.

"His wife and daughter died?" she asks in disbelief.

"Yeah. I just don't know how anyone could get over that. Anyway, I saw the sadness in his eyes when he first opened the door."

"Maybe he's not over it," Connor says.

"Of course he's not," Willow affirms. "But he hides it well."

We continue down the hill with less talking this time. I step over the limb with moss again and see the 'Theden' sign.

"This reminds me of the woods behind my grandparents' house," Willow says dodging the twigs with the bike. "I used to go there when—"

Willow suddenly stops speaking. I look at her, and she has an expression on her face I haven't seen from her, yet. She looks... in love. I follow her gaze and see it pointed at Ned.

"Connor named it Ned," I say pointed at the big beautiful

wooden giant.

"Well, then, I love Ned." Willow speeds off to Ned as we run after her. Willow hops off her bike and stands at the base of Ned looking up in awe. Connor and I catch up still huffing. The leaves are green and full, except the right side, which has a big branch missing maybe from a storm or something.

I motion up the tree. "Go ahead, Connor. Show her how it's done."

We climb through the tree like we are ten-years-old all over again. It's nice not trying to be cool for a change. I am able to be myself, which is maybe a little nerdier than I thought. We find a sturdy branch at the top where we sit with Willow in the middle.

"This… this is the most beautiful place I've been to," Willow says in a half-trance looking out at the vastness.

"Really?" Connor asks. "But, haven't you been to other places on vacation?"

"Yeah, I've been to the Grand Canyon."

"Grand Canyon? And, this is better?"

Willow smiles. "I expected the Grand Canyon to be big – so many expectations, but this … this is unexpected. Besides, it's hidden, no tourists. It's like a really good song you discover before it becomes popular."

We sit in silence in the presence of beauty.

"I want us to be friends forever," Connor says softly.

"I'm OK with that." Willow puts an arm around Connor.

"I'm OK with that." I put an arm around Connor and Willow, but mostly Willow.

We vow to stay friends all through high school; a vow that at the time, we thought would be possible to keep.

Chapter 6

"I am Coach Rider. Welcome to two-a-days. We practice two times a day: 7 a.m. and 4 p.m. We need to practice twice as much at the beginning of the season, because we need twice the preparation. Three months of lying at the pool and playing on your phones has made you all soft! That's fine if you're trying out for the golf team, but this ain't golf! Nobody is trying to knock your head off in golf. We practice in the rain. We practice in the sun. We practice in the snow. The next four months will give you a new appreciation for the comforts of modern heating and cooling.

"There is something about football that makes it all worth it. It's why young men are willing to suffer. The greater the sacrifice, the greater the pride, respect, and glory! And when a couple thousand fans are rooting for you, the Friday night lights are shining overhead, and when you have 48 teammates on the field and on the sideline who have gone with you through hell and back, and they have made you redefine how you think of the word 'brother,' then, *then*, you will know *why* you are a Jaguar football player!"

The entire team exploded into cheers, pumping their

arms high in the air like an army infantry walking onto the battle field. It's the middle of August, the first day of football practice just before the beginning of the new school year, and I . . . know . . . no one. The players are overall bigger, way bigger, than what I am used to. Maybe that's because I'm used to eighth graders! Coach Rider is the varsity coach, and he has a crazy look in his eyes. You know he loves it; he lives for it. He is about my height with a big belly. Overall, he isn't intimidating physically, but something about that short black buzz haircut and eyes of a five-star general convinces me that he means business.

"STRETCHING! Let's go! Let's go! Upper classmen: show everyone how it's done. Lines! Lines! Tyson and John, take the front!" Coach orders, waiving his clip board and jogging onto the field. He has a grey school polo tucked into black athletic shorts that stop just above the knee.

I follow everyone like one of those baby elephants you see trailing behind on the National Geographic channel. We aren't allowed to wear full pads on the first day of practice, only helmets. Tyson and John must be seniors. They are at the front, leading stretches. I follow along with everyone else while trying to blend in. Tyson is tall and slender. Maybe he is a wide receiver or something. John is shorter but built like a truck... must be a lineman.

"1, 2, 3, 4..." everyone shouts out each ten-count stretch.

Coach Rider blows his whistle, making me jump. I never

heard a whistle blown so loud before.

"Offensive, individuals! Quarterbacks, over there! Running backs, over there! Receivers, over there! And, linemen, over there!" Coach barks the orders like he's directing traffic.

I follow the other quarterbacks while sizing them up. There are seven of us. Four are taller and bigger, and one is a little taller than I am. The last one is small and skinny.

"My name is Coach Garrett, but you can call me 'Coach G.' I'm also the head freshman coach. Let's start on some footwork! Line up, arm's length apart."

Well, there's my coach, and he seems like the coolest one here. He's about 6'3" tall, black, and built like he actually played pro. He's probably in his late 20s.

"Hey, what's your name?" the smaller quarterback asks me while getting into position.

"Lawson, you?"

"Gabe. You a freshman?"

"Yeah."

"Me, too."

Gabe doesn't seem like much of a football player, more like a golfer; nothing against golfing, though. Gabe seems nice but a little squirrely. We do the footwork drills, which are easy for me since my previous coach was a stickler about them.

"What's your name, son?" Coach G asks, walking up to me.

"Lawson, sir!" I quickly reply as I continue doing the footwork.

"Good footwork, son. You new here?"

"Yes, sir!"

"Fantastic, we could use some new talent."

Coach G continues walking over to Gabe.

"You ready for the big league, Gabe? You're in high school now. This ain't slow pitch, son."

"Yes, sir!" Gabe replies, trying his best with the footwork.

"That 3-step drop needs to be tighter and quicker, son. Come on; pick it up!"

Coach G walks over to the upper classmen.

"Well, there goes my chance of playing quarterback," Gabe replies out the corner of his mouth when the coach moved out of earshot. "Oh well, I'm sure the team will be better off."

"Ah, we're all on the same team, right?" I respond, even though I, like him, don't want to be the bench player.

"Yeah, well, you'll make a good backup for us."

"Backup?" I ask.

"Tony is the freshman starter. He's really good." Gabe is looking at the guy slightly taller than me. He had short blond hair and broad shoulders.

"Water break!" yells Coach Rider.

I follow the other quarterbacks to the water, and Tony walks over to me.

"Hey, man, you must be new. What's your name?"

"Lawson. I'm a freshman."

"Yeah. Me, too. I'm Tony. We should have a good team this year. The other four guys play JV and varsity. They don't talk much, not to us at least. Your footwork looks good. Keep it up."

"Thanks!"

It feels good making a friend, but suddenly I felt like I might not be playing much.

The rest of practice went well, except for the conditioning part at the end. Coach Rider had us bear crawl the length of the field, do 50 burpees, and then bear crawl back. That's the thing about football; it will break you. I heard that's what they do in the army, too. They say it humbles you and teaches you to lean on each other. All I know is I can barely lift my arms above my head.

"Laws!" Tony runs up to me. "I'm calling you Laws, okay?"

"Okay, only if I can call you, Toe."

"No, you can't. Besides, Laws is tough. Toe is stupid. Hey, why don't you get here 30 minutes early tomorrow, and we'll throw to each other?"

"Okay, sounds good!"

"Cool, see you at 3:30." Tony walks toward a guy in a shiny new black Ram 2500 truck, must be his dad.

Wow, at least I have a friend who is cool. I walk to dad's

gray truck and hop inside.

"How was it?" Dad asks.

"Well, I made a friend with the freshman starting quarterback."

"Uh oh. Is he good?"

"Yeah."

"Well, maybe he will play up to JV."

"I don't think so. The upper classmen quarterbacks are like on 'roids or something."

"You never know. A lot can happen in a season. And remember, it's not just about this year; it's about the next four years."

We sit in silence, watching the houses go by.

"Hey, I wanted to tell you that your mom's anxiety and depression is getting worse."

"What? Why?"

"We don't know. Mental health is a strange thing for some people. Her doctor is increasing her medication, but in the meantime, she is having a hard time even leaving the house. I have to go back to work after I drop you off, but maybe you can give your mom some company."

I get home and head straight to Mom's room. She's still in bed.

"Hey Mom. It's, like, 10:30..." I say, walking over to her bed. She rolls over and pushes her hair out of her face.

"Hey, sweetie. I'm not feeling too good." She stares up at

the ceiling and then closes her eyes.

I sit on the end of her bed.

"You just tired or something?"

"It's hard to explain. Sometimes it's a completely exhausted feeling, but a very... sad feeling, like I have no motivation or happiness. Other times... I feel very uneasy, like scared, and I want to hide... I'm sorry."

Mom starts tearing up and rolls over with her back facing me.

"Hey... hey, it's okay, Mom. Dad said you're on a different medication." I pat her leg gently.

Mom rolls back over and reaches her arms out.

"Give me a hug, sweetie."

I lean over and put my arms around her.

"You're my baby... my only child. I'm so proud of you." She wipes a tear from her eye. She looks exhausted and so sad.

"Oh, gosh... I forgot." She says, covering her face with her hands. "How was practice?"

"Hard. Very hard. And, they said today was a 'light' day. But... I think I'll be okay."

"You *will*. You will baby..." She rolls back over.

"I'll be down soon, okay?"

"Okay, Mom."

I go back downstairs and check my phone. Connor wants me to come to the pool at 11, but I am thinking about my mom and the book *The Giving Tree*.

I text back: "Sorry, I need to stay here with my mom. She's not feeling well."

It almost feels unnatural for me to say. It is not as if I was never of help to my parents, but no one is asking me to stay back with her. Still, it feels like the right thing to do.

This place is a mess. Moving boxes still line the wall of the dining room, dirty dishes fill the sink, and a hamper of dirty clothes rests next to the couch. I guess this reveals how little Dad and I help with cleaning the house. Now that Mom isn't feeling well, the house is falling apart. I begin cleaning the kitchen and doing laundry. Suddenly, I start to feel more love for my mom. Huh. Maybe it's true that the more love you give, the more you have. Finally, at 11:00, Mom comes downstairs in her robe to get something to eat.

"You cleaned the house?" she says softly, somewhat in shock.

"Oh, yeah. No problem."

She forces a little smile. "Thank you."

The rest of the afternoon, I just watch movies with Mom and munch out of the fridge. She seems most like herself when she is watching a movie. An occasional scene makes her laugh, but not much. I guess it allows her to escape from her brain for a moment. When the movie ends, she is back to being gloomy. 2:15 comes, and Mom drives me back to practice.

I wave goodbye to Mom and walk up to Tony, who is waiting by the trash cans, messing with something in his duffel bag.

"Laws! Let's pregame, man." He looks around and then pulls out a couple of beers.

"I grab these from my stepdad's fridge. Here." He says, holding one out.

I look around the parking lot. No one.

"No one gets here for another ten minutes, so we're good."

I stand there, looking at the beers and not knowing what to do. I mean, I drank a beer last year at a friend's house. I know it's illegal, but it feels even more wrong right before football practice out in the open.

"Nah, I'm good. You can have them."

"Come on, Laws. We're not in middle school anymore."

"Naaahh," I say, shaking my head and trying to be cool about it.

"Well, you'll drink eventually. Everyone does." He pops them both open. "Fine with me."

He chugs them both in a matter of seconds.

"Ahhhh… Okay, let's do this!" he shouts, tossing the empty beer bottles into the trash.

He tosses me a ball, and we walk to the field.

"So, you were good at your old school?" he asks, letting out a burp.

"Yeah, pretty good, but we had a weak line, so I got sacked

a lot."

"Not here, man. Our line is strong! It's our backs and receivers who are a weak."

We throw back and forth for the next 15 minutes as players and coaches trickle in. Tony has a strong arm, accurate too.

"See," he says to me as we walk to the fieldhouse, "this is good, because coaches see us practicing. They eat that stuff up." Tony puts his arm on my shoulders, making me feel like I'm his little pet.

Practice is pretty much more of the same from this morning. When it comes time for conditioning, it was back to the bear crawls. My entire body aches, and I can hardly breathe. This is miserable. I'm so out of shape. Coach Rider blows his whistle.

"Gentlemen... we have something to discuss."

Although he has sunglasses on, you knew there wasn't a good look underneath.

"One of our coaches found something in the trash can up the hill: two beer bottles. Now, I know that no one has been on this field since this morning. THAT MEANS... it is someone, or more than one player, from this team."

Everyone looks around at each other. Tony catches my eye and slowly shakes his head as if to say, "Don't say anything."

"Now, this is how we're going to do it. You will spread out arm's length, and I will walk by each of you. YOU will either give me an answer as to whose bottles these are, or you will say, 'I don't know, Sir.' The truth is that someone knows, so if *everyone* says, 'I don't know, Sir,' then someone is lying. We are only as strong as our weakest link! Now, you don't have to say it out loud. No one will know, and if you confess, it will go easier for you. BUT, if no one gives me an answer… the whole team will do two more sets of bear crawls the entire length of the field."

The team moans.

"Someone better speak up!" John 'the truck' yells from down the line.

"OK… here we go. Everyone, quiet!" Coach Rider makes his way slowly down the line, leaning his ear into each player. He gets to Tony, pauses, and keeps going.

"Look straight ahead!" Coach Rider shouts.

He slowly makes his way toward me. What should I say? Seriously, what should I say? What if I lie and say that I don't know, but Tony already told the truth. They saw me throwing with Tony, so they would know that I know. What if Tony blamed it on me? It would be my word against his; the current starter versus the new kid. Did he plan this to get me kicked off the team? What if I tell the truth? Tony would hate me, probably bully me… but he would be kicked off the team or suspended or something. I would be starter…

I don't have time to think all this through. Coach is two players away. What do I do? What do I do? My heart beats as if I am already guilty.

I heard the player next to me whisper, "I don't know, sir."

My turn.

Coach leans his ear in. I could feel his intensity. I have to say something. I have to say something. I have to say something!

"I don't know, sir."

I just blurted it out.

He keeps walking.

I can practically hear my heartbeat. What did I do? Was that the right thing to say?

Coach finishes down the line and jogs to the center of the field.

He stands there, just staring at us with his hands on his hips. Finally, he was about to speak.

"Bear crawls!" He bellows, blowing his whistle.

The whole team grumbles. I remember what John said; 'Somebody better speak up.' What if he finds out I lied? I feel a fear I had never felt before. We lumber down the field on our hands and feet. By the last set, most of the team is crawling in pain, barely moving to the finish line. I finally collapse into the end zone. I don't know what would have been worse: this or telling the truth. Despite the exhaustion, I hurry to get my things and leave, because I don't want to be hanging around in the locker room. All the parents are waiting in the parking lot.

"Tough practice, huh?" dad asks, still looking at the field. "Extra conditioning?"

I don't want to tell him anything.

"Yeah."

When I get home, I feel like throwing up from the conditioning, but even more from the guilt. I don't know who to talk to without risking my innocence.

Brad.

After dinner, I jog over to Brad's house and knock on the door.

No answer.

I knock again.

No answer, and then I realize his Durango isn't in the driveway. I didn't even notice at first.

Willow. I have to talk to Willow.

I call her.

"Hello?"

"Willow! Hey, can you talk?" I say while sitting in Brad's driveway, not wanting to go home.

"Yeah, you okay?"

"Yeah, well, not really." I explain everything to her. I explain how Tony offered me a beer, but I didn't drink it, and then how I lied about it.

"Is that all of it?" she asks.

"Yeah."

"Well, you need to go to the coach tomorrow and tell the

truth," she says plainly.

"But, what about Tony being mad at me? Besides, the upper class would really kill me then, because they would know I lied."

"Yeah, but they might find out anyway and kill you even more for being chicken."

"This is not good."

"Did you talk to Brad?"

"No. He's not home—wait, he is now!" The headlights of a vehicle approach the driveway and kept going down the street. "Never mind, not Brad."

"You know, Lawson, the good thing about telling the truth is you never have to remember what you said. But, when you start weaving lies, you can get tangled up—"

"Sounds like something Brad would say ...."

"No, I saw it on a poster in the Library."

I chuckle. "Well, you make it sound better."

"Listen, Lawson, what if you tell Tony that you need to do what's right and tell the truth, but you're willing to do it together?"

"Why do I have to do it? I didn't even drink."

"Yeah, but you lied…"

I let out a big sigh and pace around Brad's yard. "There's no good option."

"Oh, there's a good option, just not an easy one."

"Thanks Willow. Talk to you later."

"Bye Lawson."

She's right. I'm a liar. The coaches and team would consider me just as guilty as Tony if they find out.

I know what I have to do.

I just don't know if I can do it.

Chapter 7

The first day of school…

Well, today is Freshman Orientation. The upper class-men won't be there, but they'll be at practice this morning.

I have to face Tony.

I eat some cereal and catch a ride with mom, who says she is going to try and make it into work today. She seems better, but I don't know how much of that is pretending.

"Today is your big day, sweetie," Mom says, pulling up to the football field.

"I'm going to do great, Mom. I'm ready." I don't want to give Mom any more stress than she already has, so if she can pretend, I can too.

"Love you," she says.

"Love you too, Mom." I give her a hug and grab my stuff.

I arrived a little early, hoping to talk to Tony like Willow told me to do. He isn't on the field or by the trashcans. The field glistens with morning dew as the sun starts to peak over the horizon. Taking a seat on the bench, I look at the empty bleachers. Coach was right. Two thousand screaming fans would make it all worth it, I guess, unless you're on the bench or the whole team hates you for being a liar. Maybe I would have been better off at my old school. I wonder what Bryan and my other friends are doing. I miss them.

I hear a car door shut. It's Tony. He spots me and slows his pace down a bit, probably thinking about his apology.

Standing up, I make my way over to him.

"Tony, we need to talk." I say, trying to be confident.

He turns away from me and looks at the field. "Yeah, I know, man."

"Are you going to tell the coaches?"

"What?" he barks at me. "Are you kidding me? I wouldn't be able to play!"

"Yeah, but what if they find out anyway? It will be worse!"

"What if they don't? It will be better!"

I shuffle my feet, trying to find a new approach.

"Look," he says, adjusting his duffel bag, "we did the right thing. Our team needs us."

"Hey, man, I didn't have to stick up for you. If I told the truth, I would probably be starting instead of you! And, it's not too late for me to tell the coaches."

Tony looks at the ground, knowing I am right.

"Yeah, well, are you sure that the upperclassmen will understand? Just because you tell the truth now doesn't change what we put them through yesterday. They're not the nicest people, you know. Last year, John sat on a freshmen's face after practice because he was mouthing off. I heard he passed out for a few seconds, because he was suffocating. The player ended up quitting and then eventually moving away, because he was getting bullied and called 'porta potty.'"

A lump forms in my throat thinking about what they would do to me. I've never been bullied before.

Tony takes a step toward me and presses his finger against my chest. "Listen, we need to stick together... okay?"

Three players are walking toward us, and more are pulling up in the parking lot.

I look at them and then back at Tony.

"Okay," I say reluctantly.

The fact is that if I turn us in, then I will have no friends and probably get bullied. If I don't, I still have a chance this year.

Tony smiles. "Come on, man. Let's get ready for practice."

I can't help but feel like I let Brad and Willow down, but maybe they just don't understand. It's easy for them to preach righteousness when they're not in my situation.

Players are murmuring about if anyone knew who brought the two beers. Tyson walks in.

"Well, good morning, ya'll! Anyone have any news for me?" Tyson asks with an evil grin curling on his mouth.

No one says anything.

A player speaks up. "It could have been just somebody walking by. I mean, there's no way of knowing if any of us was here between practices."

"Maybe you're saying that, because it was you!" Tyson says, stepping up to him, his reddish blonde hair and green eyes seeming to catch fire.

"No! It wasn't me!" The player shudders.

Tyson walks over to me, but I keep pretending to be messing with something in my bag.

"You. Who are you?"

I look up slowly. "Lawson. I just moved here."

"You like to drink long necks before practice?" Tyson was grinning, hoping it was me.

"No…" I say, looking back into my bag trying to not sound like a liar.

"Wait a second." He moves closer to me. I can feel his energy like a dark, demonic shadow coming over me. "Didn't I see you and Tony throwing the ball before practice?"

I pause.

"Yeah, we were throwing around."

"Hey! Was anyone here before Tony and this new kid?"

No one replies.

"Well, well, well. Looks like we might have our boys, then!" Tyson gathers people around for the execution.

"Tyson, hey, it wasn't us man," Tony speaks up confidently. "I was throwing with him, but it wasn't us." Tyson looks at Tony, trying to fish out any weakness in this testimony. Tony just looks back with the best acting face I've ever seen.

Everyone waits in complete silence to see what Tyson will do.

"Well, darn." Tyson leaps over to Tony and puts him into a headlock, swinging him around playfully. "I guess we'll still have to be friends, huh?"

Tony gives a nervous smile, trying to play along.

Everyone goes back to what they were doing.

I might have peed down my leg a little…

It is the first day we can hit with pads. Coach starts practice showing us how to properly tackle. I usually play safety on defense, so I am already a good tackler.

Coach G lines us up for open-field tackling drills. "Move toward your opponent while chopping your feet. Aim for his inside hip and focus on his belt. The head, feet, and hands can fool you, but not the belt. Drop your hips and tackle your partner with your head up and across his body. Shoot out your hands, drive your feet, wrap up, and take him to the ground. Got it? Ok, here we go!"

Ethan, a freshman lineman, is up against a JV player. He's probably knocking on 200 pounds, which is impressive for a freshman, but most of it is fat. You know the saying 'fat and happy?' Well, that's Ethan. He's always smiling until he wants to knock your lights out. Ethan is the tackler in the drill, and the JV player is the runner with the ball. The tackler is supposed to be in a three-point stance: two feet and one hand on the ground, ready to explode forward.

The whistle sounds. Ethan busts forward, but the runner jukes him at the last second, avoiding the tackle.

"Keep your feet underneath you, Ethan! Next!" Coach G yells while pacing beside us.

Same runner, different tackler; Gabe is up.

The whistle sounds. Gabe gets a hold of the runner, but he slips out of his grip. No surprise there.

"Nope! Next!"

It is my turn. I step up and get into the three-point stance. My eyes are on his belt. I can get this guy.

The whistle sounds. I run forward and start chopping my feet, waiting for him to make his move. He jukes left and then right, but I'm on him. Drop hips, shoot hands, drive feet… We collide hard as I take him to the ground.

"Now, that's a hell of a tackle! Atta boy, Lawson!" Coach G cheers, pumping his fist at me.

I jog back to the line. Tony gives me a smirk. I can't help but smile back.

That felt good. Real good.

People say football is a dangerous sport, and they're right. It can be. I knew a kid who actually became paralyzed from a hit. Concussions are also serious. But, I think most of the problems come in college and pro when people are bigger and faster.

We clean up and walk across the parking lot to the school. It's the first day! High school! I can't believe it. I walk with

Tony and Ethan. Ethan doesn't know about the beers, and neither of us offered to let him in on our little secret.

"You know how they say that being a freshman is the worst year for guys, because all the girls want upperclassmen?" Ethan chuckles while pushing his curly hair out of his eyes. "Well, I figure not for me, because I'm as big as most of the upperclassmen. So, shoot, I might be having senior girls coming to *me*!" His voice booms even as he speaks casually.

"Ethan, what's up with your hair, man?" Tony asks, pulling a strand back in front of his eyes.

"I grew it out!"

"And, that's a good thing?" I ask.

"Well, that's because I'm big and beautiful! They even make departments for me in stores." Ethan flicks his hair back with his fingers.

"You mean big and tall!" I say, laughing.

"BB! Your new name is 'BB'! Big and beautiful!" Tony says, jumping up and down.

"I fully embrace that." Ethan starts moaning while rubbing his body.

Tony pushes him away. "You're nasty!"

"It's okay, BB" I say. "He calls me 'Laws.'"

"Yeah, that name sucks. It's not big or beautiful." Ethan says giving me a wink.

"Here we go!" Tony says, looking up at the school as we approach the front door.

"Wait!" Tony shouts, jumping in front of us. "Once you walk in, the school year begins, and you have no control. Lawson, you might become a geek, and we will never talk again. Ethan, you might get really fat, and… wait… never mind—"

Ethan shoves him out of the way as he opens the door. "Your walk might always be bigger than your talk… I mean… your talk might—"

"Duhh derrr duhhh!" Tony teases.

"Whoa…" I exclaim looking up at the tall glass ceiling. We stand in a big open area with the office on our right and hallways leading in three different directions. To the left is a staircase leading up to the second level, which has an over-looking balcony.

Today is freshman orientation day, so it's only freshmen. We are lead to the gym for an assembly. *Gorgeous.* The basketball court is freshly painted and polished with bleachers on all sides. And, the smell! That basketball gym smell is right up there with the 'Chinese food candles.'

Tony is talking to, what seems like, everyone. Ethan is talking to a girl. I just take a seat. I miss my old school and thinking about what they are doing. Do they even miss me? I mean, I get the whole "challenging yourself at a bigger school" thing, but at least, there, I know I would have been happy.

"Ninth graders take a seat! Take a seat!" A Student Council

girl announces over the microphone. "We're about to begin."

She must be the school president. I look for Tony and Ethan but can't find them. They must have sat with their other friends.

"Lawson!" A voice squeaks from behind me. I turn to see Connor a few rows back. He gets up and makes his way to me.

I'm actually happy to see him since I have no one to sit with.

"Hey," I say, scooting over for him.

"Where's Willow?" I ask.

Before he can respond, I see her. She is beautiful. Black shorts, a gray tank, and a big smile.

"Hey kids," she says, walking up the bleachers to us.

"I'd sit with you all, but you're not cool enough, so…" she teases, strutting past us toward her girlfriends.

Why is she *so* hot?

"Okay, freshmen. Who is ready for high school?" the president announces, walking across the gym floor.

Most people cheer, including Connor.

"Welcome to Mill Valley! My name is Char, and I am your Student Council President. Your high school experience starts today, and it's up to you to make it whatever you want. Whether you want to excel in sports, academics, extracurricular activities, or all the above, the next four years await you. We will be going over how block scheduling works and other policies. Then, we will finish with a relay race and a performance from our pep band!"

Char is a tall Asian girl and apparently a great public speaker. She seems nice. As she carries on about the policies, I see Willow out of the corner of my eye. She is twirling her straight blonde hair and chewing gum. Her friends aren't as pretty as she is. In fact, they don't seem like the cool kids. She really doesn't seem to care about all of that. I wish I had her confidence. I mean, I'm confident… when I have friends and am starting as quarterback.

"Time for the 'freshman relay!'" Char shouts. "I need six guys and six girls!"

Some students raise their hands, including Connor, but most students don't. I don't blame them. It seems kind of corny to me. Char starts picking people. Willow doesn't have her hand up, and neither does Tony. Ethan is practically jumping up and down, and yep, he just got picked. Char starts moving toward my direction. She is looking at me. Why is she looking at me? I'm not raising my hand.

"Okay, both of you!" she yells.

Is she talking to me and Connor? I look up at Connor, who is motioning with his hands that we're a duo or something.

"Did you just volunteer us?" I ask Connor, wanting to strangle him.

"Yeah! Come on! It will be fun!"

Before I can respond, he is already on his way down.

This is not happening. This is not what I had in mind.

Char gives the instructions. "Okay, you three guys and you three girls are one team, and the rest of you are the other team. One guy and one girl on each team will start by doing a human wheelbarrow to half court. The next couple will do leap frog from half court to the end of the court. The final couple will do a three-legged race all the way back. Choose who will do what now."

Our team consists of me, Ethan, and four other people I don't know.

Ethan takes charge. "Okay, Jamie and I will do the wheelbarrow race. Connor and Sarah, you do the leapfrog, and Lawson and Britney will do the three-legged race. Come on, let's win this!"

No one argues with Ethan, and I don't think we have a choice. I look at the girl he called Britney. She is tall and muscular, like maybe she plays sports, like all of them. She also has a crazy look in her eyes like she's very competitive.

"Britney?" I ask, pointing my finger at her.

"Yup. Are you good at the three-legged race?"

I thought about the last time I even tried—maybe in 5th grade or something.

"Oh yeah, no problem," I say as if it's something I do in my spare time.

Britney has curly black hair, green eyes, and a thick wrinkle between her eyes like she is mad or really focused. She's almost as tall me and probably as strong.

"Everyone to your positions!" Char shouts.

"Ready…"

A Student Council member ties our legs together.

"Set…"

Why is this happening?

"Go!"

The crowd cheers as the wheelbarrow couples lumber toward half court. Ethan is holding Jamie's legs, and they are flying. They easily beat the other couple, and now it is Connor and Sarah doing the leap frog. They're almost here, and the other team is still wheel barreling.

"Go!" Britney yells as Connor and Sarah pass us.

Britney lurches her inside left foot as I move my outside left foot, causing us to nearly fall. I try to keep up and take two big steps. We hobble completely out of sync, trying to figure each other out.

"Stop! Inside foot. Ready. Go!" Britney shouts at me as if I am her little sister.

We got on the same foot, but our tempo is off.

"Speed up!" she shouts.

"Just take longer, slower steps," I reply.

We are approaching half court, and I look over my shoulder to see the other team starting. They are moving and gaining on us quickly.

I step on Britney's foot, rolling sideways, falling to my

knees, and bringing Britney with me. She rolls on top of my back with our ankles still tied together.

Britney screams in agony right in my ear causing it to ring. The sound of a Britney's stomach turning howl makes the whole gym silent as we lie on the floor and she holds onto her knee in agony.

I close my eyes, trying to make all of this go away. A teacher rushes over, and someone shouts, "Get the trainer!"

Some student council members are trying to untie us, but Britney is acting hysterical, which makes it hard. I can tell that I didn't completely sprain my ankle; just a tweak. Finally, they untie me, and I slowly get up not knowing what to do. Do I sit down, or do I help? I just stand there looking down at Britney who is grimacing in pain and clenching her teeth. Coach G comes running over and helps the trainer pick her up and carry her off. Some people are cheering, but most people are still in shock. I slowly make my way to the bleachers and notice every eye in the gym on me. My face turns red and hot. I don't want to walk all the way back up to my seat and receive the berating of each person I walk by. Noticing an open seat in the first row, I slowly walk over to it and sit down.

"Geez, well, we hope she's alright…" Char says getting back on the microphone.

"Well, thanks anyway for everyone who participated… umm…" Char turns and looks to a teacher who is telling her something.

"Oh yeah, OK, and now a performance from out pep band!"

The band starts playing, but no matter how loud the percussion and trumpets are, they don't seem to drown out the awful feeling still in the air and the sound of Britney's tendon still popping in my mind. I can feel the people sitting next to me emotionally moving away, like I'm plagued with embarrassment. I crack my knuckles relentlessly, making my way around each finger. *People are noticing. Act normal.* How? I just twisted a girl's leg off in front of all my almost friends. I stare at the lines on the court, waiting for it to end. As the band finishes, I stand up with everyone else moving toward the exits. I look down at my paper… history… Mr. Wright—

"You okay, man?"

I look up and see some guy I don't know.

"Yeah… uhh… not sure what happened…"

"Yeah, that was crazy. Coach Hicks isn't going to be happy."

"Coach Hicks?"

"Yeah, the soccer coach. Britney is goalie and was expected to play JV or even Varsity."

No. Why is this happening? Now, everyone is going to think it's my fault and hate me.

"I tripped on her foot and rolled my ankle," I say, trying to explain myself.

"Haha, yeah and your team was doing so good, too!"

"Thanks," I say, wanting him to go away.

"Okay. See ya," he says, finally leaving.

I nod and start moving in the direction of the doors.

"Lawson, are you OK?" Connor comes running up. I want to punch him.

"Why did you volunteer us?" I say under my breath, trying not to scream.

"I'm sorry! I thought it would be fun."

"It wasn't, and now I look completely stupid."

Tony comes up behind us. "Lawson! Haha, that was awesome!"

"Awesome?" I ask.

"No one likes Britney—well, except for the soccer team. She had it coming."

"Okay," I reply, still feeling guilty.

Connor walks off.

"Hey… are you friends with Connor?" Tony asks, looking over his shoulder as Connor walks out of sight.

"Yeah. We met this summer in my subdivision."

"Hahaha! He is such a dork! So awkward—"

"Hey, he's a nice guy," I say, defending Connor.

"Sure, yeah… I'm just trying to look out for you. I mean, your first impression with everyone, so far, is wiping out on the gym floor and hanging out with Connor. That's a rough combination!" Tony says laughing, slapping me on my back and then walking off to talk to some girls.

Tony is a freakin' jerk, but he's right. Everyone probably thinks I'm a loser now.

"Hey," Char calls out as she walks toward me. "I'm sorry about what happened."

"Oh, yeah. Me too," I reply somewhat shocked that she is even talking to me.

She wrinkles her nose, feeling pity on me. "Just don't let this ruin your day," she says. I look at her eyes. They're genuine.

"Okay, thanks." I reply, thankful but now hoping everyone will finally stop paying attention to me.

"Hey, you should think about trying out for Student Council," she says, nudging my shoulder.

"Oh, yeah. I bet I'll win now."

"Well, at least everyone knows you. Now, all you have to do is be nice to people." Char goes her own way, and I head to history class…

I follow the map on my cheat sheet and walk into Mr. Wright's Human Geography class. The best part of this class… Willow. The room is set up with sets of four desks facing each other. Seeing Willow in the back corner, I walk over and sit in front of her. She smirks, pretending I'm not there.

"Human Geography. This course teaches the earth's regions, religions, languages, governments, ecosystems…"

My teacher is quite possibly the most monotone person on the planet. How is that possible? He doesn't even look that old. I can, kind of, understand if he is, like, sixty years old and has been teaching for 35 years. Who wouldn't be monotone by then?

I'm going to write Willow a note. Tearing off a sheet of paper, I write at the top, *"Stop playing footsie with me..."* I slide it over.

She writes back. *"I'm not, weirdo."*

"Maybe it's the guy next to you," I reply.

She reads it and almost laughs.

"Shouldn't you be sulking or something after what happened to you this morning?" she writes.

"You will employ spatial concepts and landscape analysis to analyze human social organizations..." Mr. Wright carries on.

I look at the piece of paper, trying to decide if I should write what I want to write. What the heck, I don't have much to lose today.

"Will you go on a date with me?"

I can't read her face. She doesn't really smile, but she also doesn't seem weirded out. She tosses me the paper. I pause while Mr. Wright looks in my direction and then back to the chalkboard.

"What do you have in mind?"

"Meet me at Ned at 7:30 tonight," I reply.

Mr. Wright continued his lecture. "You will also learn about the methods and tools geographers use…"

She doesn't write back. Does that mean no?

She grins and looks at the teacher, and suddenly, I feel a foot tapping against my leg. She lifts her hand just above her desk and points to the guy next to her.

I'll take that as a 'yes.'

It's a half day. I go to my other classes and then head to lunch with Tony and Ethan. Connor stays over by some other people, but I'm not sure if they are even his friends. I feel bad for not sitting with Connor, but I'm still mad at him for volunteering me.

When school gets out, Mom is waiting for me in the parking lot.

"Hey Mom," I say sliding in the passenger seat.

"Hey sweetie." Her voice is flat, and I notice she's wearing her sweats. I guess she was too tired to even change clothes.

"So, I met I girl I like." I say knowing it would cheer her up.

"Really?" Her voice slowly regains some life. "What's her name? Does she like you?"

"Willow, and yes, I think she does."

"Aww, see I knew people would like you here," she assures me clicking the blinker and pulling out of the school.

"Yeah, we'll see," I reply, letting the hum of the vehicle

saturate the side of my head.

When we get home, I talk to Mom and Dad a little more and then get ready for Willow.

Man, what a day, I think to myself while walking down to Ned. I start getting worked up over Connor again, thinking about how stupid he was to think I'd be cool with that.

I don't care, though. I have a plan for tonight.

Willow and I had become good friends over the summer. She, Connor, and I hung out at the pool and down at Theden Road. Maybe I'm moving too fast. I have a tendency to do that in relationships, but if I don't act now, someone else will.

I look down at my bag full of everything I planned for Willow. I want it to be special.

The weather is perfect: not too hot with a light breeze blowing through the trees. At 7:00 p.m., I walk up to Ned and start thinking about my plan. Setting my bag on the ground, I get to work. Half an hour later...

From the top branch, I watch as Willow walks down the road in blue jeans and a t-shirt. Her hair is up in some kind of Indian hippie braid. As she gets closer I see her smiling.

She's beautiful, like, in a natural way. Emory was pretty also, but I don't know, something is different about Willow.

Emory bends over and picks up my first note.

Ned and I want to tell you how amazing we think you are. Ned has three notes for you as you make your way to the top.

She is grinning ear to ear as she walks up to the first

branch, trying to peek up at me.

She read the note on the first branch…

1. You are nice to dorks and strangers who read children's books.

Her smile grows as she climbs to the next branch.

2. You don't care about what people think, are you are so confident and know who you are.

Next tree limb…

3. You're beautiful.

She climbs the last couple branches up to where I am sitting.

"Are you trying to be romantic, Lawson?" she says slowly, sliding next to me.

"Don't get your hopes up," I reply, handing her a cup.

"What is this?"

"Decaf tea from Pat's Coffee, and I got myself a decaf coffee."

"You *are* trying to be romantic. Mmm… thank you," she says, holding the cup with both hands while taking a small sip.

"So…" I try not to let my giddiness show. "Today was…"

"Bittersweet?" Willow tilts her head and nudges my side.

"Yeah, bittersweet," I agree taking a sip of my coffee.

A bird lands on the limb next to us, maybe a sparrow, or something.

"Birds don't worry much do they?" I ask watching it

bounce from limb to limb.

Willow takes a sip. "I guess not."

"They don't have to worry about popularity... or bullying... or scary female soccer players."

Willow laughs. "I don't have to worry about those things either."

"You've never been bullied?"

"Well, OK when I was in sixth grade some of the popular girls started spreading rumors that I had fleas—"

"Fleas?!"

"Yeah, which I didn't! But, I guess the boys in the class started liking me, so they had to come up with something."

"What happened?"

"Well, it was easy for me. I just told them I wasn't interested in their boys and they didn't have to worry."

"You let them win?"

"No. I wasn't even playing. They wanted something that I didn't care about. Yeah, I know people should stick up for themselves sometimes, but I guess it didn't bother me enough. I mean, my friends knew it wasn't true, and they were the ones I cared about the most."

"So, you don't wish you were a bird sometimes?" I ask watching it fly away.

"Mmm... No. I love birds, but I like being human better."

"Why? Humans are awkward, insecure, mean... well, all humans except you apparently."

Willow takes another sip and smiles as if she has something to say.

"What?" I ask.

"I can be insecure, maybe not mean, but insecure."

"You? You're the least insecure person I know. What are you insecure about?"

She looks at me inquisitively like she is impressed I was brave enough to ask her that.

"I mean, you don't have to answer that," I say retreating me question.

She holds her cup with two hands and smells the aroma. I'm entranced by her charm, her poise. She looks at me with her nose still in her cup. Her eyes grab me. "I'll tell you if you tell me first."

"What I'm insecure about?" I ask.

"Yup."

I fidget on my limb looking out at the sun sinking down, tapping the tops of the trees.

"I didn't think about this question being flipped."

Willow laughs and grabs my hand. I see her hand on top of mine with her fingers wrapping inside my palm.

"It's OK if you're not brave enough."

"I'm not brave enough," I say, smirking.

Willow nudges me again.

"Hey! No nudging thirty feet up!" I say letting my giddiness peek through.

"I mean, you don't have to answer that," She mocks me with my own words.

"No… no, I'll tell you. Not that I'm overly insecure or anything."

"Right."

"It's not even worth talking about."

"Definitely."

"Fine… I guess I'm insecure about the thought of being unpopular. Like, I was popular at my old school and everything was certain—"

"And now?"

"Now, everything is uncertain."

"Everything?"

"OK, well, not everything."

"What are you certain about?" She asks scooting closer.

"I'm certain that Pat makes good coffee, and…"

"And tea." Willow adds.

"Yes, and I'm certain that Brad is the coolest old guy I know."

I laugh and squeeze Willow's hand.

"And I'm certain that…" I look at her calming soft blue eyes. "I'm certain I really like you."

Willow whispers in my ear, "Really? I couldn't tell."

Her breath from the "t" in tell gives me chills up my side.

I struggle to keep my composure. "Well, I just want to let you know how I feel before some other guy does… and well,

I want to know if you want to be my—"

"*Choo! Choo!*" a train blares its horn as it rounds the corner, cutting me off.

Willow starts laughing and nearly spills her cup, "AWW, AND YOU WERE DOING SO GOOD!" she shouts in pity.

"*Choo! Choo!*" the train barrels past us.

"*I SAID, I WANTED TO KNOW IF YOU WOULD—*"

She kisses me.

Lip gloss.

"*Choo! Choo!*"

She leans back, smiling and nodding before taking my hand inside both of hers. We continue to sip our tea and coffee as we watch the train roll by. She rests her head on my shoulder as the sun sets behind the trees.

I fell for a girl named Willow high up in a tree named Ned.

Chapter 8

My alarm wakes me from a deep sleep. I pull myself out of bed and into the shower. It's Friday and the first real day of school. All the upperclassmen will be there. As I step into the shower, I stop midway and remember what happened last night.

"Woohoo!" I say aloud, doing a little dance in the shower. "I got a girlfriend! I got a girlfriend!"

Wait. Emory.

My thoughts shift to what she might be doing. Is she mad? Is she sad?

Oh no! She said I could message her after the first day of school, and I never did!

I was so caught up with what happened yesterday and then with getting ready for Willow. I just forgot, but I have mixed feelings. I miss Emory, and I even feel guilty as if I was cheating on her, but I didn't. We're moving on, right? OK, maybe I'm moving on faster. But, the thought of her being with a different guy makes me jealous. I can't think about that. Besides, today is the first day of real school, so I can text her tonight.

I finish getting ready and go to football practice. Most people like me now—probably because Tony likes me. Gabe also likes me, but I feel bad for him, because I know that he will never play. No one brought up the beer bottle thing again, so it looks like I am in the clear.

On my way into school, I pull a small dandelion from the grass along the sidewalk and head inside to Willow's locker. She is already there, pulling her books out. I slide in behind her locker door and stick my arm around it, holding the dandelion.

She grabs my hand and the flower. "My boyfriend brought me a weed. Aww… I'm so lucky."

I step out from behind the locker and wrap my arms around her waist. She couldn't hide her smile as she took the flower weed and put it in her hair.

"First day of school," I say, with my arms tightly around her waist.

"And, so it begins." She smiles, looking up into my eyes. "You have a little green in those brown eyes," she says, noticing for the first time.

"You have a little gorgeous in those blue eyes."

She squeezes me tightly and kisses my cheek. "You're cheesy… and I like that."

"Get to class, freshman," she orders, walking away like a football player.

I grab my things and head to first period Language Arts.

We have block scheduling here, meaning that we only have four classes a day, but each class is about an hour and a half long. So, today will be my first four classes, and then tomorrow will be my other four classes. They use the school's colors to keep them straight. Today is a silver day, and tomorrow is a blue day—seems completely complicated if you ask me. How am I going to keep that straight all year long? Then the whole ninety minutes of each class seems almost unbearable, but they say it saves time compared to the usual fifty-minute classes, because less time is spent settling in and wrapping up.

"Come in everyone! Come on in!"

Oh yeah, Coach G is my teacher. Sweet! I see Connor is motioning for me to sit by him.

"What up, bud?" I ask, sitting down.

"What's up? What's up? You and Willow, that's what's up!" Willow must have told him.

"Yeah, are you okay with that?"

"Yeah. Well, you guys seem to like each other, so... I'll allow it." He cracks a smile and then opens his notebook and writes down today's date.

"Oh, no!" I mutter. "Britney is in this class."

She pivots through the door with crutches and a cast.

Dang, I really messed her up.

Connor leans over and whispers in my ear, "Did you ever apologize to her?"

I shook my head.

"Well, are you going to?"

I nod my head. "I'll do it after class."

Britney makes eye contact with me, but before I could look away. She gives me a look that says, "You're a dead man."

Geez, maybe Tony was right about her being crazy.

"Welcome, everyone, to language arts! I'm Mr. Garrett, and I'm the coolest teacher at this school," he says, writing it on the board and getting a laugh from the class.

Mr. Garrett turns to the classroom. "Seriously, that will be on the test."

Some girls seated in the back of the room giggle.

I bet they have a crush on him. Coach G is a cool guy. He's good looking, buff, and talks normal, unlike my Human Geography teacher, Mr. Wright.

"We will be reading and analyzing several books this year, starting with *Animal Farm*. If you love anarchy, you will love George Orwell's *Animal Farm*, because the animals take over the farm, but then struggle to maintain order and equal rights among themselves. OK! Now, we are going to do a little ice breaker this morning to get to know people. With most literature, you have character development. This is the description and readers' comprehension of the characters in the story. So, table one, pair up with table three, and table two, pair up with table four."

I look down and see that we were table three and then

look over to table one.

"Son of a—"

"Britney. Britney is at table one," Connor whispers, as if sounding the alarm for me.

"Well, I guess now's my time to apologize for something that wasn't my fault."

We get up and head toward table one. She is sitting with her soccer friends. Wow, this is amazingly awkward. The girls are talking to another guy and girl seated at the table, but they say nothing to me or Connor.

"Okay. I want you to start by sharing your characteristics with each other," Coach G instructs.

Our group looks around, waiting for someone to go.

"I'll go!" Britney pipes up.

"Well, my name is Britney, and I'm a girly girl," she says sarcastically, tossing her hair. "And, I play goalie in soccer… oh wait… I did until I did a three-legged race with that idiot right there."

A couple of her friends giggle, but everyone else stays silent.

"Oh, and now I wear this sexy cast, so that's another characteristic. What about you Clementina?" she says, motioning to her friend next to her.

"Well, my name is Clementina and—"

"It wasn't his fault, you know," Connor says to Britney, interrupting Clementina.

"Are you serious?" Britney asks, furrowing her eyebrows.

"He didn't mean it."

"You mean, he didn't mean to be born half retarded?" Britney's other friend asks.

"You know," I say, finally chiming in, "I felt really bad about what happened, and I was going to apologize, but now I'm kind of glad it happened."

Britney scowls at me like she is planning my murder in her head.

"You're gonna wish it didn't," she says wiping off whatever fake smile she once had.

"Okay, everyone. Back to your seats. Hopefully, you know a little more about each other and..."

Britney's words stay with me: "You're gonna wish it didn't."

Was she serious? Would she actually do something crazy? She looks like she would.

One thing is for sure, I think Connor is making my life harder for me. If he didn't volunteer me, none of this would be happening. I get how he was trying to defend me in front of Britney, but that just enraged her even more. I need to say something.

After class, I stop Connor by the water fountain.

"Hey, Connor. I need to say something."

"Look, I know. Just don't worry about her. Okay?" Connor says, interrupting me.

"I'm more worried about you!" I blurt out.

Connor falls silent.

"What do you mean?" he asks, confused.

"You! If you hadn't volunteered me, none of this would have happened. And then in there… you just pissed her off even more and created this big drama," I say, raising my voice.

"I was just trying to stick up for you," Connor says softly.

I feel myself getting worked up.

"Yeah, well, stop trying, because you're making it worse! You might be used to not having friends, but I'm not!"

Connor quickly walks off without saying anything.

I immediately feel bad. I know I was too rough but come on! This is the next four years of my life we're talking about, and Connor is doing a lot of damage in the first twenty-four hours!

I walk to my locker, and Tony comes strutting over to me.

"Laws! Hey… Laws, Ethan and I are going to a house party at Liam's tonight. You should come. It would be a good way for you to create a better name for yourself."

"Who's Liam?"

"A junior. He doesn't play any sports, but he's a cool guy."

"Okay, I'll ask my parents when I get home. Can I bring my girlfriend?"

"Whoa! Girlfriend?" he asks, dancing around me.

"Yes. What you never heard of one of those?" I ask,

grinning and pushing him away.

"Who is it?" he asks.

"Willow Harrison."

He stops dancing and raises his eyebrows.

"You know her?" I ask.

"Yeah," is all he says, and I know instantly that he likes her. "Yeah. That's cool," he continues. "But here's what you need to tell your parents. Just tell them you want to take her to eat at Figlio's Restaurant, and then walk to the movies next door. But instead of dinner and a movie, you will come to Liam's house, because it's, like, 5 minutes away. Parents get all weirded out about house parties and stuff."

"You want me to lie to them?"

Tony gives a three-finger Boy Scout salute. "Yes, sir, I do!"

"I don't know, man. Will there be drinking? Aren't you worried about getting caught?"

"Umm… no. It's not like we're parading around town with shot glasses. It's just a party, and that's what you do in high school."

"I don't know…"

"Hey, it's cool. Forget I even mentioned the party. Besides, you two probably already have plans to play Monopoly or something with Connor."

"Will there be any other football players there?"

"Yeah, several upperclassmen. Look, I'm just trying to help you out, man."

Tony is right. I need to make a better name for myself, and it sounds fun.

"Okay. I'll ask Willow."

Tony starts dancing again as he walks away.

I see Willow at her locker.

Seeing she doesn't notice me, I sneak up behind her and kiss her cheek making her jump.

She quickly turns around. "Hey!" she says, laughing. "You scared me."

"Do you want to go on a date with me tonight? Dinner at Figlio's and then a movie?"

"Wow! You're so sweet. Okay. Sounds like fun." She grabs her books, and we start walking.

"I'll have my dad drive us there, and we'll pick you up at 7:00."

"You sure know how to treat a girl." She blows me a kiss as she turns to walk to class.

Technically, I'm not lying. I'll tell her about the party when we get to Figlio's, and if she doesn't want to go, we don't have to.

I walk into Mr. Thomas' Biology class and take a seat. It's an advanced placement class for mostly sophomores. One girl is seated on each side of me.

"Hey, what's your name?" the girl on my right asks.

"Lawson, I'm a freshman."

"Hey, Lawson, I'm Sydney. Wait. Someone told me about

a new kid named Lawson who tore Britney's knee during—"

"Yeah, that's me," I say quickly.

"Oh, my gosh! I bet that was so embarrassing!" She leans a little closer toward me and says, "You're kind of cute for a freshman."

I look at her and then quickly look away. She's pretty—curly black hair and dark clothes.

I grin and feel the heat on my face. "Thanks."

"Do you have a girlfriend?" Sydney continues, resting her chin on her hand.

"Um… yeah, I do." My face must be beet red by now.

Why am I being so shy? I guess I'm not used to girls being so straight forward.

"Bummer. Now I can't flirt with you. It's okay, we can still be friends," she says, smiling and turning around to talk to someone else.

I look around the room as if to say, "Did anyone else just see that? A sophomore girl wants me!"

OK, maybe she does that to all freshmen guys … but maybe not.

The rest of the school day drags on, probably because I keep thinking about the party tonight. Part of me is really excited, and part of me is nervous. What if there are drugs or something else illegal going on there? What if I get caught at a party where there is drinking? Would I get kicked off the football team?

Mom picks me up from school. She isn't her chipper self; must be the depression again. During our drive home, she barely says a word.

"Are you okay, Mom?"

She looks at me and then back at the road. She's wearing sweats and a t-shirt, her eyes saggy and sad.

"I'm guessing you didn't make it into work again today? Are you okay?"

"I'm just…" She pauses, lets out a big sigh, and then tries to smile. "I'm sorry, sweetie. I'm just going through a tough patch right now with this depression."

"Is the medication not working?"

"No… no, it's not," she says, half focused on me and half lost in thought.

"Well, can they give you something else?"

"Yes… I guess they can."

Geez. I've never seen Mom this bad, and I don't know what to do.

"Do you want to hear some good news?" I say, smiling.

She forces a smile. "Yes. What's your good news?"

"Willow and I are going out."

A flash of light flickers in her eyes as she briefly comes to life. "Honey, that's so cute—I mean, that's great! I'm happy for you. You really like her?"

"Yeah!"

"And, do you still miss Emory?"

Emory! I need to text Emory. Gosh! Why do I keep for-getting about her? I was crying over her not that long ago, and now she's barely on my mind.

"Actually, no… not really," I say, surprising myself.

"Good. I'm glad. You two are moving on," she says, pull-ing into the driveway.

"So…" I say. "Can I take Willow to dinner at Figlio's and then see a movie tonight?"

"I'm sure that will be fine." She unbuckles her seatbelt and opens the car door. "Just ask your father when he gets home."

Mom pushes herself out of the car and walks to the house like she has been up all night. I want to say something to make her feel better, but I don't know what to say. She heads straight to her room.

Likewise, I go up to my room to text Emory.

It's so weird texting her again, like I'm bouncing between two worlds. Maybe she's over me and doesn't even want to talk.

I still need to text her.

Me: "Hey! What's up? How was your first day?"

I wait a few seconds. No response. I start feeling jealous thinking that she might have a new boyfriend. I make my way to the bathroom when I hear a new message alert.

Her: "Good, and you're not going to believe this…"

Me: "Believe what?"

Her: "My mom got a promotion in Kansas City, and I think it's the same part of town you live in! Looks like I might be moving too! CRAZY!!!!"

My heart sinks. What about Willow? No!

My phone alerts another new message.

Her: "Lawson?"

Me: "Wow, that's crazy... when?"

She doesn't reply for a few seconds and then starts typing...

Her: "Just kidding. I wanted to see what your response would be. Apparently, not too excited, which tells me all I need to know..."

What? Kidding? I let out the breath I was apparently holding in. Part of me feels relieved, and another part feels mad for being tricked.

Me: "How can you lie about something like that?"

Her: "Sorry. My day was good too. Bye."

And that was it. That's all she said. I don't want to reply. I feel done with the whole thing. She's trying to pin me as the bad guy, and I just can't stand that. I know what she's doing. She's playing games.

I don't reply back, and neither does she. Maybe it is best that I moved. Emory and I were bound to get in a huge fight and blow up on each other sooner or later.

Trying to shake off Emory, I do some homework. About an hour later I hear the door shut and Dad's size twelve shoes walking through the kitchen.

"Dad!" I shout on my way down the stairs. "Hey—" I cut myself off when I see his face.

"Yeah?" he asks leaning over the island with tense shoulders and a stern look.

"Whoa. You OK?"

He turns around and leans against the island with his arms crossed. "Yeah… just a stressful day."

"Sorry, Dad." He must appreciate my sympathy, because he turned back around to face me with softer eyes.

"Hey," I continue. "Can I take Willow on a date tonight to Figlio's and then a movie?"

Dad smirks and I see his 14-year-old inner child break through. "You got a girlfriend?"

I poke my chin in the air. "I sure do."

"Dude."

"So, that's a yes?"

"Well, yeah! My man! What's her name? Tell me about her!" He says sitting on a stool.

"It's Willow from—"

"This summer! Yes!"

Whenever Connor, Willow, and I bumped into Dad over the summer, Willow was always quick to strike up a conversation. Dad likes that.

"Yeah," I continue. "She is smart, pretty, nice—"

"And, she likes YOU?"

I chuckle, impressed with Dad's attempt at sarcasm. "Nice," I reply walking to the island.

"I'm kidding. Of course she likes you. You have good genes," he says winking, but in a creepy way. "So, you want me to take you two on a date, huh?" he adds.

Dad's question triggers a flashback. Mexican Restaurant. Movie. Emory. First date.

"Dad, what did you think of Emory?"

"You guys were really close... I liked her, but... Ahh never mind—"

"Tell me."

Dad gives me a second to change my mind and then looks up at the ceiling grabbing his chin. "She..." He cautiously says squinting his eyes. "She was... well, she could be at times..."

"Controlling?" I ask grinning.

Dad laughs. "I was going to say she was a firecracker, but—"

"Remember how she rearranged my room?"

Dad laughs harder. "Yeah, well, your mother does that to me all the time."

For a moment I feel close to my dad, like we're friends without all the parental weightiness. Why did we grow so far apart? Why can't we talk like this more often?

"But, yeah," Dad says getting up from his stool and making his way to the stairs. "I'll take you two tonight.

Besides, you need all the help you can get."

"Don't help. It's… nope." I shake my head as Dad tries hiding his cheesy grin up the stairs.

He slips me a $50 bill.

"Thanks, Dad!"

"Hey," he says, smiling, "perks of my promotion."

As we pull up to Willow's house, the first thing I notice is the yellow. The front door is sunny yellow like a beacon shining into the neighborhood. The house itself is soft grey and a little smaller than my house. It sticks out from the surrounding house. The features are unique. Window box planters spill over with white flowers. A smile grows on my face. It's a perfectly suited house for a girl who stands out in a world of brown.

"Okay, let's go meet my future daughter-in-law," Dad says, getting out of the truck.

"That would be way down the road, Dad. Also, don't act weird in front of her parents. Okay?"

"I wouldn't even know how to act weird," he says, waddling like a duck.

The door opens, and Willow is wearing a pink dress and heels. Uh, oh. I realize that I'm just wearing jeans and a t-shirt. Well, it's probably because I'm thinking house party, and she's thinking fine dining.

"You look… amazing!" I say.

"Thanks!" she replies, looking at my sub-par outfit.

Her parents come out from the kitchen, and her dad approaches my dad.

"Hello! I'm Doug, Lawson's father." He shakes hands with Willow's dad. "You must be Lawson's future in-laws. Just kidding! Just kidding!"

What the heck, Dad.

"I'm just joking," Dad says, bringing it down a notch. "But, you do have a wonderful daughter."

"Thank you. We are both very proud of her." He turns to his daughter and wife and then back to Doug. "I'm Gary, and this is my wife, Shelly." Shelly steps closer and shakes hands with Dad. Gary is a big, burly guy who has balding hair and a big beard. He seems nice. Shelly has a class to her. I guess that's where Willow gets it from. Shelly has blonde wavy hair and is wearing a summer dress with pearls, but something is off; she's missing that glow in her smile and twinkle in her eyes that Willow has.

"We have heard only good things about Lawson from Willow, and she is very picky with guys," Shelly adds and then smiles at Willow.

This is my cue for trying to make my best first impression while feeling hypocritical about my undercover plan, so I extend my hand toward Mr. and Mrs. Harrison. "Nice to meet you, Mr. and Mrs. Harrison." *Yeah, Mr. and Mrs. Harrison, I'm actually a compulsive liar who wants to take your daughter out partying.*

"I'll bring them both back by 10:45—I mean, I'll have Willow back by 10:45." Dad laughs and points at me. "Lawson stays with me."

I hope they don't judge me by my dad.

We walk to the truck, and I open the back door for Willow—not forgetting to be a gentleman. I slide in next to her.

"You are so funny, Mr. Peters," Willow giggles.

"See, Lawson?" Dad looks in the rear-view mirror at me and then to Willow. "You need to convince Lawson of that!"

I pat Dad on the shoulder. "I'm just jealous, Dad."

I look over at Willow. She is gorgeous. But, she's not just pretty. She is intelligent, kind, and she has an energy to her that's calming and exciting at the same time. How did I get so lucky?

Dad drops us off and says he will pick us up at the theatres at 10:30.

As Dad drives off I contemplate on how I'm going to sell the whole idea of going to a party in heels to Willow.

"Hey," I say, grabbing Willow's hand.

"Yeah?" she says, looking up at me with those big blue eyes.

"You look gorgeous."

"Aww. Thanks, Lawson." She slips me a kiss on my cheek.

I wanted to say something about the party but totally chicken out.

"Peters, party of two," I inform the hostess, feeling ritzy. Figlio's isn't a super fancy place… well, yeah, it's pretty fancy.

We are escorted to a table with a candle on a white linen cloth.

I let Willow take her seat first. That's one thing I'm really glad Dad taught me. When I was young, we went to a couple of fancy restaurants, and he always demonstrated proper etiquette. You always pull out the chair for the lady or let her sit first if it's a booth. Put the napkin on your lap as soon as you sit down. The silverware is set up to use, starting from the outside in. So, the salad fork is on the far left and the soup spoon is on the far right. Then, the dinner fork is on the inside left and the knife is on the inside right. If you get up to go to the restroom, you always place your napkin on your chair. When you're finished, place your napkin left of your plate, but not on your plate.

Willow puts her napkin on her lap and sees that I did the same.

"You're more refined than I thought, Mr. Peters," she says in a haughty voice.

I give her a wink. "As are you, Miss Harrison."

"Have you been here before?" she asks.

"No. Have you?"

"Yeah. The baked ziti is awesome."

"Good evening. May I get you two something to drink?" the waiter asks, interjecting.

"Yes, and I think we're ready to order," I say, trying to hurry along the process.

"Willow?" I ask, knowing that you're always supposed to let the lady order first.

"I'll take a peach iced tea and the baked ziti, please."

"And I'll have the same."

The waiter nods and walks off.

"So…" I say, trying to casually bring up the party. "Tony told me there is a party five minutes away. I was thinking we should check it out. What do you think?"

"And skip the movie?" she replies, confused.

"Yeah. We can always see a movie another time. It will be fun."

"But, our parents don't even know about this."

"It's only five minutes away, and it's not like we have to drink or anything."

"There's drinking there?"

"Yeah. But there's several football players there, and—"

"I don't know, Lawson. Besides, I'm too dressed up."

"You look beautiful! I would be proud to show you off."

She blushes but is still unsure.

"Really? Is that why you want to go—to show me off?"

"Yeah. You know the other football players will be there, and… I don't know… I'm just so proud to be your boyfriend."

"But what if our parents ask us what the movie was

about?"

"It's a superhero movie. They're all the same: good guys, a lot of fighting, and the good guys always win."

"I don't know..."

"Come on, it will be fun. Please? If you don't like it, we can come back to the movies."

"Well, okay, if you really want to go."

I relax into my seat knowing I pulled off the plan.

The waiter sits our drinks down.

"Cheers," I say, lifting my glass. "To the prettiest girl and the luckiest guy."

"Don't forget it, either," she says, clinking her glass against mine.

When our food comes, Willow lets me take the first bite, because she wants to see my expression. "Mmmm. What the *heck* is this? Oh my, gosh! Mmmmm," I say again, closing my eyes and leaning back in my chair.

"I told you—the best!" Willow says, probably a little too loud, which draws attention to our table. We fed each other bites, because that's what people do in romantic movies. It's kind of funny, though, because we both ordered the same thing.

"What you did for me at Ned was..." Willow pauses trying to find the words. She smiles and taps her food with her fork. "No one has done anything like that for me."

I want to tell her I love her, but I don't want to freak her out. I'm bad about rushing things.

"I really put you on the spot, didn't I?" I ask putting my fork down.

"You mean if I said no to wanting to be your girlfriend?"

"Yeah, I mean, can you imagine the awkward climb down?"

We both laugh catching more attention in the restaurant.

"Wow, I really did put you on the spot, huh?"

"I wanted to be put on the spot." Willow winks just before stuffing a big bite of steamy lasagna in her mouth.

I love this girl.

"So, your parents seem cool. Do you get along with them both? What do they do?"

"Oh," she says finishing her bite. "Dad is a plumber. He's really good, and Mom is a financial advisor at the bank, but…"

I wait for her to continue.

"…but the funny thing is she doesn't manage money well. She loves shopping. So, every time she goes, she brings me something—which I like but, I guess it's like how an alcoholic doesn't like drinking alone. My dad argues with her about it a lot."

Willow's mood changes, and I can sense the sadness she has for her mom.

"What about your parents?" she asks trying to regain her usual pep.

I lean back and cross my arms. "Well, Dad is a 7Up plant manager—"

"Really? Cool!"

"Ha! That's the most enthusiastic response someone has ever had to my dad's job title."

Willow laughs. "Well, it's cool! I guess it's because my parents never really let me drink soda growing up. So, in a way, it's like your dad is a rebellious mobster drug dealer, or something."

I bust out laughing. "Rebellious mobster. You have my dad completely wrong."

"And your mom?"

"Oh, well, Mom used to be a lunch lady and a bus driver at my old school, but she's having a tough time right now…"

"You can tell me if you want," Willow says gently.

"She has depression, and it's been getting worse."

Willow doesn't say anything.

"It's getting worse. So, she hasn't gotten a new job, yet." I stare down at my plate.

"Hey," Willow says softly making me look up at her.

I've never had someone look at me with so much compassion.

"You don't have to be ashamed."

I look away.

She's right. That's exactly what I am, ashamed.

"I can tell that you love her, and that's all she needs from you. You're not a doctor. It's hard, because, sometimes, I want to fix Mom, but I have to keep telling myself. I'm not a psychologist. I'm her daughter. So, I just need to love her."

She reaches over and grabs my hand.

I start to fidget my feet under the table. I feel uncomfortable, vulnerable, and at the same time... loved.

"Thanks," I say, finally. "Wow, this was amazing, right." I gesture at the food trying to transition away from my discomfort.

"And, it was such a treat." She winks, hinting that I'm paying.

I nod in agreement. "Yes, ma'am!" I pay up, and we head to Liam's house. I open the door for Willow, and as we step outside I can see the movie theatre across the parking lot. I open the address on my phone and follow it around the theatre. As we pass the theatre I feel both convicted and exhilarated. We arrive to see several cars parked along the curb, and some people are hanging out by the front door. I text Tony, and in a matter of seconds, he pops out.

"Laws!" Tony suddenly notices Willow. "Willow Harrison," Tony says, crossing his arms.

"Tony," Willow replies, flatly.

"Nice dress. Hey, what do you see in this guy?" Tony nudges me playfully.

She puts her hands on her hips. "Quite a lot."

"Well." He starts laughing. "Just don't do a three-legged

race with him, huh?"

Tony steps to the side. "Come on in; come on in. I'll introduce you to Liam."

I wonder if Willow ever had anything with Tony. Just the thought makes me a little sick.

We walk inside to see about thirty people standing around in the living room, kitchen, and on the staircase.

"When's the big match, Lawson?" Ethan shouts from the kitchen with a beer in his hand. I look at him and have no idea what he means. "You and Britney!" he says, boxing the air.

Is he serious? Is Britney saying she wants to fight me?

The smell of weed hits my nose. I never tried it, but I was around it once in middle school with my friend's older brothers. Even though it's legal in certain states, it's still illegal here. I'm not sure where I come down on all that. I'm definitely against smoking cigarettes. All those gross pictures they showed us in elementary school of how smoking causes cancer in your mouth and blackens your lungs must have done their job.

"Come on. I'll introduce you to Liam."

We follow Tony and pass a couple making out in the kitchen. Suddenly I feel like I'm in one of those high school movies. A loud bass sound echoes from the basement.

I spot on older guy, maybe a junior, checking out Willow as we pass by. She doesn't seem to notice, but I can tell she is a little nervous about this place from the look on her face. I grab her hand as we step out onto the back deck.

"Liam, this is my second-string: QB Laws and his girl, Willow."

Liam turns around, wearing a pirate hat and holding a beer in one hand and a joint in the other. He's a good-looking guy, maybe Hispanic, and stocky.

"Laws, what's up, homey?" Liam flashes some made-up gang sign. "Welcome to mi casa, bro, and… my, my, my, what a lovely lady you brought with you tonight. It's a pleasure, madam…" Liam bends over like a pirate-knight greeting a princess.

"Hey," Liam announces, opening his cooler, "have a beer."

He holds two out for me and Willow. I glance at Willow to see what she would do.

"I'm good. Thanks though," Willow says politely.

"Well, I never push a lady," Liam says, putting the two beers in front of me. "But I always push my bros to be their best!"

I stand there looking at the beers, not sure what to do. Will Willow be mad if I drink? Will Tony and Liam think I'm stupid if I don't?

I take the beers.

"Thanks, man," I say, following orders and popping one open.

"*Yessirrrrr!*" Liam makes a pirate face and wraps his arms

around me and Tony.

We hang out on the deck, talking for half an hour, as I make my way through my second beer. Willow seems okay, but I can tell that she is just putting up with it all. Meanwhile, I feel myself loosening up. The guys seem to like me, and all the worries of being a loser for four years seem to have been a false alarm.

We go back into the kitchen and almost get tackled by Ethan, who comes out of the kitchen like he is running a blitz. He grabs my arms and starts wrestling with me.

"You better toughen this boy up for his match with Britney!" Ethan says to Willow.

I pull myself off and start laughing. "Wait. Are you serious? Does she really want to fight me?"

"Dude, she *haaates* you, and she has her soccer minions planning to kill you," he says, waddling around pretending to be a minion.

"Seriously?"

Ethan was making inaudible minion sounds and crazy faces.

Maybe it's the beers, but suddenly I don't care about anything. I see a roll of duct tape on the kitchen counter and get a wild idea.

"Hey everyone!" I shout, setting my beer on the table. "Three-legged race around the house! Who wants to take me and Willow on?" I shout again, raising the duct tape in the air.

People laugh and holler—apparently all wanting to join in.

"He wants to break your leg, too, Willow! He's a serial three-legged killer!" Tony shouts at Willow while stabbing the air.

Willow laughs and is willing to go along with the ride. She kicks off her heels as I wrap her leg and mine together before passing the tape. Everyone is joining in. There are about twenty-two people huddled in the kitchen with their legs tied.

"Okay!" I shout. "On my count, we race around the house and back here. Don't break anything!"

"Like a tendon!" someone hollers from the back, making everyone laugh.

"3... 2... 1... Go!"

We hobble through the hallway, people bumping into each other and laughing hysterically. I hear a slight crash behind me immediately followed with, "It's okay!" and more laughing. We round the corner toward the living room, and I feel a big hand on my shoulder pulling me and Willow back. It's Tony paired up with Ethan bounding past us.

"No fair!" Willow shouts.

We all collapse in the kitchen, laughing our heads off. I look at Willow, who is laughing, and for the first time, I feel like this is my new hometown. All my fears and insecurities seem distant as these seemingly strangers are now laughing with me. I'm accepted. People like me. I have Willow.

We tell everyone goodbye and make our way back to the movie theaters. I put my arm around Willow as we walk through islands of light on the darkened road.

She hands me a piece of gum. "You might want this to cover up your breath."

"I'm not drunk or anything," I say, laughing.

"I had fun, Lawson, but you know that's not my kind of thing," she says, looking at the darkened houses as we walk.

I look at her and then at the road. "I know. Are you mad that I drank?"

"I'm not mad. I just… the whole popularity thing and needing to drink to have fun just seems a little… sad."

"Seemed fun to me," I say, smiling.

"It's also illegal, and you're risking a lot with football and stuff, but I'm not trying to be your mom or anything. Look, I'm just not into the whole sneaking around behind parents' backs and stuff. Okay?"

"So, you're never going to hang out at a party again with me?"

"Not one where we have to lie and risk getting caught."

"But, it was fine. It wasn't too crazy, and our parents will never know."

"I just like to live a more honest life."

I don't know what else to say. Does this mean I can't go to

a party even by myself? How can I have friends? I don't want to spend all my high school days hanging with the dorks and playing board games on Saturday nights. I don't want to have to choose between partying and Willow, but it feels like that's what she's making me do. Maybe she'll loosen up more as the year goes on. I mean, I don't want to get into trouble either, but as long as I'm smart about it…

Still feeling the adrenaline of the three-legged race, I scoop Willow off her feet.

"My name isn't Lawson. It's Bob. I'm an undercover cop, and I'm taking you to jail for lying to your mother!"

She squeals. "Oh my gosh, let me down!"

"You've seen too much; you're coming with me now!" I grunt, stumbling through dark pathway.

We both laugh and hold hands as we walk into the theater parking lot.

10:15. Right on time. Dad should be here any minute.

"Oh yeah! The movie! Super heroes, right?" Willow asks.

"Yes, ma'am! The good guys win in the end."

"Evil always loses… remember that, Mr. Peters," she says, tapping my shoulder.

"Oh, are you the angel on my shoulder?"

"My name isn't Willow. It's Betsy, and I'm your guardian angel."

"Betsy? How did you come up with Betsy?"

"Because, it's awesome," she says, laughing.

We sit on a bench in the front of the theaters for a few minutes when dad's truck pulls up. I open the car door for Willow.

"I taught him all his manners!" Dad proudly announces.

I jump inside and close the door.

"So, how was the movie?" Dad asks.

I wink at Willow. "Great! The good guys win in the end," I proclaim confidently.

"They always do," Dad says, nodding his head. "Well, I'm glad you two had fun. And how was dinner?"

"Mmm, the baked ziti is my favorite," Willow says from the back.

"Good! So, tell me, Willow…"

Dad starts interviewing Willow with a hundred questions all the way back to her house. I stick my arm out the window, feeling the warm breeze and watching a million stars glimmer in the clear night sky.

I'm a high schooler.

Maybe this big city move will work out after all.

Breeze slips through my fingers.

So many stars.

Chapter 9

"Ribosomes synthesize protein for secretion," Mr. Thomas lectures from the front of the room.

This biology stuff is harder than I thought.

Sydney—the sophomore who was flirting with me—still flirts with me in class. She bumps elbows with me and taps her foot against mine. She leans over to me and whispers, "I hear you're becoming 'Mr. Popular.'"

It's true. Ever since Friday night at that party, my phone has been blowing up with friend requests and notifications. I'm not going to lie; it feels really good. People I don't even know pass me in the hallway and say, 'What's up, Laws!' I guess that nickname is permanent now.

I shrug and flash my phone showing all the friend requests.

"Hot," she mouths.

Willow would hate Sydney if she knew how she flirts.

When school gets out, I head to the fieldhouse for football practice. Our first game comes up in just a few days. Coach has me playing wide receiver, which I'm actually okay at.

"Blue 42! Blue 42!" Tony calls out the cadences. "Hike!"

Five steps forward, turnaround fake, and head straight to the end zone. One, two, three, four—

The sound of someone screaming makes everyone stop. It

was an agonizing sound coming from the line of scrimmage. Just from the type of scream, you knew it was bad. All the coaches rush onto the field.

It's Tony.

Sprawled out on the turf just five feet behind the line of scrimmage, Tony grabs his ankle in anguish as he bites down on his mouth piece while letting out moans.

"What happened?" Coach G yells as he quickly makes his way to Tony and gets down on all fours.

Everyone is listening. "I… I rolled my ankle. Must be… broken," Tony wails.

Coach G and a trainer pick up Tony and carried him off the field.

Players murmur. "Oh, no…" "There goes our season." The thought hits me: I'm the backup.

I should be excited, right? I mean, this is what I've always wanted, but Tony is better than I am. If I mess this up, everyone will hate me again. Maybe Tony will hate me for taking his position. My mind races with anxiety. I haven't studied the plays like Tony has. What if I forget a play?

"Lawson!" Coach G shouts, jogging back onto the field.

Everyone looks at me.

"We need you to step up, son. You ready?"

"Yes, sir!" I lie.

"Okay. Good! Wedge Right 42 Blast to start you off easy."

Wedge Right 42 Blast is a quick handoff to the running

back. I know this. It's a common play that everyone learns in youth football.

I start to jog over to the huddle when Coach says, "Lawson…"

"Yes, Sir?"

"Show confidence for the team."

"Yes, Sir!"

I jog back to the huddle, trying to put coach's advice to practice by faking as much confidence as possible. The skeptical eyes of ten players beam on me like a laser as I wedge myself into the huddle.

"OK, guys, Wedge Right 42 Blast on one. Ready?"

"Break!" everyone shouts in unison.

Walking up to the huddle as quarterback, I feel in my natural environment, but this time it's a different town, a different team.

"Blue 42!" I start the cadences, forcing out a loud, deep voice, hoping I wouldn't squeak halfway through.

"Blue 42! Hike!"

I squeeze the ball with all my might to prevent the dreadful snap fumble, turn around, and shove the ball into the running back's belly. Rolling out, then showing a fake, I turn to see him bust through an opening, gaining five, six, seven yards. Juking a safety, he keeps going. Players start cheering. Ten, fifteen, twenty yards!

Touchdown!

"Yes! Yes! Yes!" I repeat in my head. Players are giving high fives and slapping helmets.

Tony.

I glance over my shoulder and see Tony looking at me before being escorted into the fieldhouse.

Is he mad at me? Is he happy for me?

"Nice blocking and running, boys!" Coach claps from the sideline.

The rest of the practice went well with the exception of only a few times when I was confused about a play, but I even made a couple of pass completions. As we walk to the fieldhouse, Ethan comes up from behind me.

"Way to step up, Laws." He grabs my shoulder pads and gives me a little nudge.

"You think Tony's out?" I ask.

"Never heard him scream like that... probably."

We all make our way over to the trainer's office to check on Tony. He's propped up on a blue table with his ankle in the air. The trainer steps out to stop the crowd. "Hey, everyone. Tony probably has a broken ankle, but we have to wait for x-rays to verify that. He just got done with some ice, and now he's elevating it. If you're going to say something, make it quick."

We all file in. Tony doesn't look happy.

"Sorry, bro. Heal up quickly, man," Ethan says as others echo their condolences.

I don't know what to say. I was nervous to even look in his eyes, as if he could read my mind about feeling happy to start as quarterback now.

"How did you do out there, Laws?" Tony asks with everyone turning toward me.

I slowly raise my head. He has a friendly smirk, but somewhere deep underneath, I sense something darker.

"Well, not as good as you."

"You did good, man," a player from the back yells out.

Tony doesn't break eye contact with me. "These boys are counting on you now. Don't let them down. And, don't get too comfortable playing my spot."

The other players chuckle as Tony's grin grows bigger.

I try my best to smile back. Being the starting quarterback must as important to Tony as it is to me, maybe even more for him. He doesn't have a girlfriend, so in a way it feels like I'm taking his girl away from him, and it's never good when you mess with someone's girl.

We shuffle out of the room and head for the parking lot. Dad is waiting for me in his truck with his phone up to his ear. I get in, and we take off.

Dad's talking on his phone. "No, it shouldn't be like that. You're right. Yes. Okay. Yes, I know. I'll fix it. Absolutely. Yes, Sir. Okay. Bye."

his tone tells me something is wrong.

"Sorry about that," he says, fidgeting with the steering

wheel.

"What happened?"

"Oh, it's the plant... my boss... well, there are some issues," he says, trying to find the words.

"Issues?"

"Yeah. Somehow, we ran a wrong part for nearly three hours today without noticing, and now... well, it's not good."

"So, you're in trouble?"

"Phillip! Phillip put the wrong part on, and he ran it! But, I'm the plant manager, so I have to take the responsibility. All I know is that I will get the boot if it doesn't get fixed."

"They might fire you?"

"Now, listen here... that... that won't happen. I'll make it right... somehow."

I can sense Dad's fear. I'm not even sure what it would mean for the family if Dad got fired. Probably, not good.

After a couple minutes of silence, he finally asks me, "How was practice?"

"Well, Tony probably broke his ankle, and—"

"Broke his ankle? What? Tony, the quarterback? So, you're starting now?"

I thought he was going to swerve off the road in excitement.

"Ha ha. Yeah, and I did well. No big mistakes."

"Well... that is great—not for Tony—but for you!" Dad smiles and then seems to retreat into his thoughts. As we drive home, I feel Dad's tension. The only other time I saw him like this was when Grandma had a heart attack about eight years ago, and we were all driving to the hospital only to find out she didn't make it. Although we didn't know it at the time, Dad had this same look in his eyes, as if he suspects the worst even as he tries to hide it. It's scary when your parents are scared, even when you're a teenager.

When we pull in the driveway and stop, Dad doesn't turn off the engine but just sits there like he wants to say something.

"Son, as you know, your mother isn't doing too good. In fact, she's getting worse—"

"What about her medication?"

"Not working. Fortunately, though, she has short-term disability, which she is starting to take. But, I'm worried about her being by herself too much."

"Like worried she will kill herself?"

"Well, no, I don't think she would, but the doctor said positive social interaction is good for her, even though she says she doesn't have the energy or interest for it."

"What am I supposed to do?"

"I don't know. Just give her a hug and tell her you love her," Dad says, turning the engine off.

We walk into the house, which is eerily quiet. There's no TV or pots and pans clanking.

"She must be upstairs," Dad says, looking up toward their

room.

I make my way up the stairs slowly.

"Mom?"

I take a few more steps up.

"In here," I hear her say softly.

She's in bed on her side with the lights off and the fan on high.

I walk over to her side of the bed and give her a hug.

"Love you, Mom."

She doesn't move or open her eyes.

"Love you too, sweetie," she whispers. "I'm just really tired."

Her eyes are closed, and I am struck by what I see. I study the wrinkles on her face and stray gray hairs on her head. My mom is getting older. It's a weird feeling knowing your parents are getting older, kind of scary. In a way, it feels like she is 90-something years old and dying. I tilt my head and imagine my mom as a little girl lying in her bed. I wish I could make her feel better.

"Let me know if you need something, Mom... I love you."

She murmurs, "I love you," back half-asleep. I make my way out of the room. It's 5:30 p.m. Why would she be this tired? I hate seeing Mom like this. Do I stay with her or give her space? It's so confusing and sad. I didn't even tell her I'm starting quarterback, because I don't want her to have to fake excitement.

I walk to my room, plop on the bed, and pull out my phone. Tony already posted pictures of his foot. I keep scrolling and see a pic of Connor with his dog. I haven't hung out with Connor since I shouted at him about Britney. Willow hangs out with him sometimes at school, though. I don't know. Maybe it's best that Connor and I don't hang out a lot. We're just in two different crowds.

After I eat dinner, I decide to walk over to Brad's house. I haven't seen him in a long time either. I guess I've just been so busy with school and hanging out with Willow.

Brad is outside putting mulch around his trees. "How nice of you to come help me, neighbor," he says, opening another bag.

"Is this $40 also?" I ask facetiously.

"I'll pay you in wisdom. I'm overflowing with it... just spread the mulch evenly around this tree."

The red mulch is warm with a rich cedar smell.

"So, do you hate high school or love it?"

I chuckle as I spread the mulch around the trunk. "I hated it at first, but now I'm starting to love it."

"Feel like sharing details?"

"Well, day one started with Connor volunteering me for a pep rally relay in which I caused my teammate, who just so happened to be the goalie for the girls' soccer team, to trip and sprain her knee or something."

"Ouch."

"Yeah, she's in a brace now."

"No, I meant for you. Rough first impression."

"Right. Then Willow and I started going out and—"

"Whoa, whoa, whoa! Back up!" Brad interrupts me with a big grin. "May I ask how you asked her out?"

"Down at the elm tree off Theden—with some notes about what I like about her, leading up to where I was sitting in the tree."

"Bro." Brad sticks his fist out for me to pound.

"Ha ha, yeah, and I've become pretty popular at school, because I went to a party and lead a three-legged race around the house... THEN, just today at practice, Tony broke his ankle, and now I'm starting quarterback!"

"Wow, too bad for him, but congratulations, my friend. You have a lot going for you right now," Brad says, grabbing another handful of mulch.

"Yeah. So, I'm doing good now."

Brad smiles and nods his head as he finishes his pile.

"So, what's your wisdom?"

Brad spreads the mulch out slowly as he prepares his words.

"Much is given. Much is required."

"I think I've heard that before."

"It's out of the Bible. You have been given a lot in a short amount of time: love, popularity, leadership. Now that you have more, more is required of you."

"Like, responsibility, right?" I ask, patting the mulch down.

"Unfortunately, when people are given more, they usually expect more… like The Giving Tree. Sometimes, the most dangerous time for an army is right after they've achieved victory. They get lost in the plunder, forget about their duty, and ultimately become like their enemies. This is a time to rejoice, but it's also a time to be cautious. Popularity, partying… you can get lost in it. I think you know what I'm saying."

"Yeah, I do. Be cautious and smart about it. I got it."

Brad smiles and looks at our finished work.

"Trees. Their roots grow deep before their trunks grow tall, because otherwise, the weight of the tree would rip the roots right out of the ground. We have to have strong roots first. Otherwise, our successes will topple us over. Pride comes before the fall. Let me ask you again, what do you want?"

"This question again?" I laugh, grabbing the mulch. "Well, I didn't start as JV quarterback, but I'm starting freshman quarterback now, so…"

"And, you like quarterback more than wide-receiver?"

"Oh, yeah, quarterback is my position—"

"Why?"

"Well, I'm good at it."

"OK," Brad says light-heartedly. "Let's suppose tomorrow you discover you are even better at the tight-end position. Would you change?"

I pause to think about it. "I don't know. Probably not."

"So, what's so fun about being quarterback? Why would you choose that even if you would be better at a different position?"

"Being a quarterback is cooler than being a tight-end."

Brad raises his hand as if I had won Bingo and looks slowly at me. "That's what you want."

"Huh?" I ask, confused.

Brad put down the mulch. "Lawson. What you really want is to feel like you're somebody. You want to feel important. You want to be popular, because you're afraid of being alone. That's why you want to play quarterback, and—"

"Wait a second," I say, getting defensive. "So, everyone who wants to play quarterback only wants to be popular?"

Brad stares straight at me. "Not everyone, but you do."

I look at him trying to see if he is serious.

"Listen, Lawson, I'll tell you straight, because this is what you need to hear. You care too much about popularity, and if you're not careful, it will tear you up."

I shook my head. "Yeah, I think I have to go."

As I stand up, Brad reaches his hand out. "Lawson—"

"No! No, it's cool, man. I have some 'homework' to do. I need to think about this big lesson I'm learning from you about being an ego-maniac."

"Lawson, hey, I'm sorry. I just—"

"You know what, Brad? Maybe you're the one who wants all the attention. Maybe you wish you were cooler, but instead you settle with hanging out with freshmen students."

"Lawson. I'm sorry! All I was saying is you—"

"It's okay; I'm sorry too!" I yell over my shoulder, not slowing down.

I thought Brad was cool, but he's starting to sound like my parents. He thinks he knows everything. Why can't he just be happy for me without all the ancient Greek philosophy crap? He acts like he completely knows me, and then he thinks he can judge me. Not cool. Maybe he was too good to be true. Maybe his true judgmental colors are coming out. Besides, does he want me to have no ambition and take the lowest positions in life?

"It's not that easy!" I heard Dad yell from upstairs as I came through the door; Mom and Dad are arguing. It sucks when parents fight. I wonder if it's about his job or Mom's depression. I thought I heard something fall over, but it could have been dad's foot stomping the floor. Is marriage even worth it? Maybe people just get annoying over time. Look at how Emory and I were falling apart before I even left, and now there's Brad's deal. Could I marry Willow? Well, I'm in love with her, but I also used to be in love with Emory…

Oh, well. I grab the T.V. remote to escape it all. Mom

shouts back, which is rare for her.

"I DON'T CARE, DAMNIT!"

Volume up.

Still fuming over Brad's words, I also feel a little guilty about storming off. Why should I feel guilty, though? People should be happy for me. Instead, I'm getting preached to by the guy down the street and brought down by the people upstairs. I feel myself going numb to it all.

As the commercials roll on, the meaningless drowns out the meaningless.

Chapter 10

"You suck! No one likes you!"" Spit flings from Tony's mouth as he yells in my face. Veins bulge from his forehead.

I take a step back, but he continues berating me.

"You know what? I never really liked you, Lawson. Actually, the only thing I like about you is your girlfriend. Maybe I'll trade you for her."

Tony pushes me hard, and I stumble backward but stay on my feet. I don't want to fight him. I am afraid to. I want to leave.

Someone grabs my waist. I turn to see Willow.

"Willow, stay back." I order, but she doesn't listen. She walks up to Tony. Tony stops yelling at me and turns his attention to her.

I reach for Willow's arm. "Willow, stay out of this."

She pulls away.

"Leave him alone, Tony," Willow says. "He's not worth it."

She grabs his hand.

"What are you doing Willow?" I ask, confused. A sick

feeling grows in my stomach.

"What? Tony asks, wrapping his arms around Willow's waist. "You didn't know Willow and I had a past?"

Something just snaps inside, and I lurch toward Tony. He grabs my shoulder, and I can feel his fist slam against the side of my head.

Blackout.

"Choo, Choo."

Opening my eyes, I can see ceiling fan blades twirling round and round.

"Choo, choo." The train rumbles in the distance.

I rub my eyes, trying to wipe away the dream.

Dreams are weird. They're so convincing. They seem like reality until you actually wake up to reality. My dreams are usually stressful and involve me running from someone or trying to find something.

The idea of Willow being with Tony really bothers me. And even though it was just a dream, I can't help but feel like Willow already cheated on me.

I check my phone and see a text from a number I don't recognize...

"Hey, Lawson. It's Char from student council. Hey, I want to let you know that freshman class elections are coming up, and I thought even though you're new, you would make a great leader. Anyway, check out the info when you get to school, and let me know if you have any questions. See ya!"

Elections? We had those in middle school, but I was never involved with that sort of stuff.

Dad is quiet during the drive to school, and so am I. The radio is also quiet. Dad always has the radio on, so he must be pissed or something. I know I should probably ask him what's wrong, but I don't want to. He's the parent, not me. We pull up, and I get out without saying a word. He drives off.

Tony is the first person I see when I get inside. He is in a cast with crutches. I immediately feel like choking him with his crutches for what he did in my dream.

He sees me coming and looks down at his foot while shaking his head.

"Well, at least it's my left foot," he says, holding it up for me to see.

"Why does that matter?"

"I can still kick your ass with my good foot if you fumble a snap," he says, half serious.

"Man, I'm sorry this happened to you. How long will you be out?"

"Too long." Tony hobbles off without saying anything else. I guess I would be mad too, but I'm not sure if he is more upset about his foot or about me taking his position.

Willow sees me and runs toward me, nearly mowing me down as she wraps her arms around my waist.

I squeeze her back. "Hey, babe. Why are you so happy?"

"Because, I love you," she says, kissing me on my cheek.

"I love you, too, babe. Hey…"

She looks up at me while smacking her gum. "What's up?"

"Char said I should run for elections. What do you think?"

"Wow, talk about confident. You just moved here!"

"Hey," I start laughing, "She said it. Not me!"

"Well, you've become quite popular. And, it's not like you'll be running for president, right?"

"I don't know. I don't know which position."

"Posters! I can make your campaign posters!" She starts jumping up and down while clapping her hands.

"Oh man, I don't know…"

She stops and looks at me with pouty eyes and puckered lips. She is absolutely adorable.

"Fine, but I get to oversee it all."

"You get to oversee it," she mocks me in a General's tone while saluting me.

"Haha, I'll probably lose anyway."

The warning bell rings, so we head to Human Geography with Mr. Wright.

Students are still taking their seats as Mr. Wright begins his morning lecture.

"Good morning, everyone. We are beginning our journey into the political factors that brought about the United States as we know it. Settlers from Europe came to the Americas for many reasons and with one of the main reasons being religious freedom. In addition to tensions with Native Americans and other establishing colonies, the migrating foreigners struggled to gain true freedom from their native country, being England. Colonists relied on trade and imports from their mother country, but as taxes increased on goods, so did the conflict. Now, who can tell me what kind of government England had in the 1500s?

"Kings," someone blurts from the back of the room.

"That's true. It was a monocracy, but over time, it gradually became a democracy with its power residing in its group of officials, called parliament. This is similar to the United States House and Congress but with some differences."

"What about the Queen of England?" the same student asks.

"Yes, there is still a position for the king and queen, but they no longer have any legal power over the land…"

I notice that Willow is into this sort of stuff, because her eyes squint a little when she is thinking deeply about something. I try tapping her leg under the table, but it must have caught Mr. Wright's attention.

"Yes, sir, Mr.…." he pauses to look at his name chart, "Mr. Lawson Peters."

Uh oh.

Mr. Wright walks over to my desk. "We all know that the United States is a democracy, but many people don't realize that it's not a pure democracy. Instead, it's a democratic republic where people vote in representatives to represent them.

This is where representatives, governors, and senators come in. Can you answer my next question, Mr. Peters? Why would a group of people want to transition from a monarchy to a democracy?"

Everyone in the room stares at me. The last thing I need is another gaff like the first day of school.

"Well… freedom."

Mr. Wright walks behind my chair and stops, "Elaborate please." He seems to be getting satisfaction from his interrogation.

I look at Willow, and she gives me a nod as if to say, "Own it."

"Well… I believe… it's within all of us to want freedom: freedom to pursue your dreams, to make mistakes, and to learn from them and to be your own person. We all need some sort of structure, right? I mean our football team, for example, needs rules, officials, and coaches to make sure there is order and to prevent players from cheating. But, the choice to play or not to play is ours, and if we win, it will be because we fought for it. And, if we lose, the blame will also be on us. I guess the same is true in school. We have the freedom to an education, but we have to study. So… a democracy is like that. It's freedom, but all freedom comes with responsibility. That's why, I believe, people prefer democracy over a monarchy, because freedom can make us into something more, while it will also require more from us… but it's worth it."

I silently thank Brad for giving me the "much is given, much is required" piece from last night.

Someone starts a slow clap from the side of the room, making everyone laugh.

"Wow, Mr. Peters. Well said. Maybe you should consider running in our class elections."

"I don't know. I'm not sure if anyone would vote for me."

"What do you think, class? Should Mr. Peters enter the elections?"

The class cheers and applauds.

Willow is smiling ear to ear.

I stand up, waving my hand to appease the crowd, and then sit back down.

Mr. Wright walks back to the front of the class and continues his lecture.

Honestly, I am surprised by the reaction and even shocked by how well my mini speech went. I was popular at my old school, but I never considered myself a leader.

After school, Willow accompanies me to the elections meeting. We are informed about the rules and told that we had to choose which position to run for. I look at all the positions: President, Vice President, Secretary, and Treasurer. And, you could also be a representative. I know automatically that I don't want to count money, and I don't like detailed work that secretaries do. I could be a representative—not a lot of pressure there. My eyes draw back to president and vice president.

Could I win either of those positions? It seemed like it from my classmates' reaction. I feel myself getting ambitious, almost greedy. What if the new kid became class president? Just the thought of it makes me stand a little taller. That would be cool.

"Hey Willow," I say, turning to her, "...should I run for president?"

"You want to run for president?"

"Did you hear our classmates today?"

"Yeah... but president?"

I look at the information sheet and start smiling.

"Lawson, just make sure you're not doing this for popularity."

I don't know what to say, because I know a big part of it is just that. Who wouldn't want the most powerful position in the class? Well, I guess a lot of people wouldn't... but I think I do.

"I'm going to run for president," I say decisively.

"OK, well, at least tell me this: Why do you want to be president?"

"Because I don't like taking notes and counting money."

"What about vice president?"

"What about president?"

"What about biting off more than you can chew?"

Willow immediately retracts her words.

"Hey, I'm sorry," Willow gently grabs my arm, "I believe in you, and if you want to run for president, I'll support you. I'll be the First Lady." She winks and softly kisses my cheek.

"I'm going to run for president."

"Lawson, what do you want your posters to say?" Willow asks, sitting on my bedroom floor, staring at the blank poster.

"I don't know. What do you think?"

Willow thinks for a second. "What do people want?"

"Money. Bribes. Good idea. Yes!"

"No."

"It's called sarcasm," I respond.

"You're right. I think your posters should be sarcastic. Think about it. Most people will go with the cheesy lame stuff, but if you do that, you won't stick out."

"Tired of lame? Vote Lawson," I announce confidently.

"Wow! Why don't you say this school sucks, and you will fix everything?"

We sit for a moment, thinking.

"I have an idea," I say abruptly, "...remember how Brad talked about oxymorons, like 'jumbo shrimp'?"

"Yeah ...."

"What about... 'Start a Quiet Riot... vote Lawson.'"

Willow smiles, "Now you're talking, but the whole riot thing might scare administration—"

"But, it's quiet!"

A new idea pops into my head, and I laugh out loud.

"Why are you laughing?"

"Well, it's always good to make fun of yourself. I mean, it can make people appreciate you. So, what does everyone know me from?"

"Oh, my gosh," Willow says, smiling as if she knew where I was going."

"Hey, freshmen... 'let's put our best foot forward.' And then have a drawing with two people doing a three-legged race."

Willow starts to jump up and down, "Or a drawing of the entire class with all their legs tied to each other!"

"Yeah, maybe—"

"Oh, my gosh! Britney is going to hate you!"

"She already does! Besides, we know she's not going to vote for me. Wait! Hey, freshmen... let's 'break a leg' together."

"Haha, yes!" I can see the excitement on Willow's face.

We make about eight posters with similar sayings and stack them against my bedroom wall.

"Are you ready for tomorrow night, Lawson?"

"You mean our first home football game?"

"No, I mean the evening news. I heard they just hired a new anchor—yes, of course, I meant your game!"

I smirk while looking out the window, "I think so..."

"You nervous?"

"I mean..."

Willow places both hands on her hips, "You mean, you're

the new kid everyone is counting on, and if you mess up, they will all hate you, and you probably won't win class president?"

I glance at the floor and then at her, "You can put it that way."

"How good were you at your old school?"

"Real good," I say, crossing my eyes."

Willow laughs, "So, you sucked."

"No! I was good… but that was a small school, and the competition was probably… not as good."

"Wow…"

"What?" I ask, looking up at her.

"No, I just realized how big of a deal this is. I mean, if you lose this game, your life will be over," she says sarcastically.

I roll my eyes.

"Seriously, I will have to break up with you and go out with Connor."

"You would!" I start laughing. "Actually, I would love to see that."

"What? You would?"

"Well, you can't kiss him or love him or anything like that, but you can help him with his stamp collections or something."

"He doesn't collect stamps…"

"Yeah, he does. He has, like, 20 boxes in his basement."

"Seriously?"

"No… but maybe."

"You're dorkier than he is."

"Not possible."

As Willow is leaving, she turns to me, "Yeah, well... hey, I want to ask you a question. If you couldn't be the coolest kid in school, and if you had to give up the quarterback position... but you still had me and Connor... would you be happy?"

"Sounds like a trick question."

Willow looks at me.

"Can I trade Connor for Ethan?"

Willow barely smiles, "You know, Connor would be there for you even if you blew the game... Would Ethan?"

"Hey, Ethan is a good guy—"

"Even if you cause them to lose?"

"Ethan is my friend!"

Willow looks away.

I look down at the bed.

"You know, you should talk to Connor. He would have liked to be here tonight."

I nod slowly.

"Goodnight, Lawson."

Chapter 11

Thursday.

Game day.

Freshman games are on Wednesdays and Thursdays, JV games are on Mondays, and varsity is on Fridays. When it is your game day, you wear your jersey to school. Number 7 is mine, but I'm not sure how lucky it will be.

"OK, right here." I tear off two big pieces of tape and hang up my first poster next to the freshman lockers.

I feel like I am doing something illegal, like drawing graffiti on the walls.

As I move to my next location, I look around sheepishly. I'm just not used to this whole 'promoting myself' thing; it seems pretty cheesy.

Two more pieces of tape and another poster will be proudly displayed on the wall by the bathrooms, next to my competitor's poster, which reads, "Vote for Greighson!"

Wow. That's original. I don't even know who Greighson is.

No way! I quickly duck behind the corner; is that Britney hanging up posters?

My fingers grip the corner wall leading into the bathroom hallway, and I slowly and quietly peek around the corner.

She has an arsenal of posters between her arm and hip, and she is fumbling with her tape. Something about her seems angry, like she would be that grumpy girl in the *Willy Wonka* movie.

I watch as she hangs her poster, making sure each one is hung perfectly. She then takes a step back and looks at her poster as if she is admiring it. Finally, she walks down the hall and out of sight.

My turn. I run over to check it out.

"Boss Britney... 4 Prez" is written in large, bold pink letters covered with a lot of gold glitter.

That's the dumbest poster I've ever seen. Do people call her that? As I round the corner toward the gym, I nearly collide with...

"Connor!" I say, caught off guard.

"Oh! Sorry, Lawson. Didn't see you there."

Connor fidgets uncomfortably.

Not knowing what to say, I reply, "It's OK. See ya."

I can tell he wants to hear something else, maybe something like, "I'm sorry for ignoring you and being a terrible friend." But, I don't say it. Instead, I say, "It's OK. See ya." I know this sounds bad, but honestly, I don't want to be his friend.

I make my way to Coach G's language class, and I sense

Connor trailing behind me. I haven't been sitting next to Connor in class. I know. I'm a jerk. Blah, blah. I walk in and see Britney and her minions across the room. I can tell she is looking at me from beneath her furrowed eyebrows. It's a weird feeling knowing someone hates you. I never had anyone, at least that I know of, who hated me at my old school. It's weird, because one part of me still feels sorry for what happened, but then another part thinks she's a crazy psycho who deserves both knees twisted, while another part is literally scared for my life that she might kill me with a shank during lunch.

I take a seat and see her whisper something to her friend who starts giggling. Britney suddenly looks at me, and I quickly look away but not before having the image of her *Grinch That Stole Christmas* smile burned into my mind.

Yup. Definitely a shank.

Ring, ring.

Coach G picks up his classroom phone, which interrupted the entire class.

"Ok… sure will. Bye."

"Lawson, the principal wants to see you."

I give him a bewildered look, and unless I hadn't heard about the Thursday gift card giveaways, this wasn't a good thing. I get up slowly and walk toward the door. Coach gives me a look like, 'You better not be in trouble.' As I pass Britney's table, I don't look but can feel the side of my face burning with stares.

Once outside the classroom, I make my way to the principal's office. What is this about? Why was I called out of class? My mind races through all the possible scenarios. Maybe Dad was in an accident. Maybe it's Mom. My heart starts beating as my imagination takes over.

I open the door to the principal's office, and the receptionist looks up. "Dr. Novak is waiting for you in his office."

She had said it unemotionally, leaving me in further suspense.

I have never been to the principal's office, so I wander down the hallway hoping his name is displayed on one of these doors.

"Back here, Lawson." Dr. Novak's authoritative voice calls from the back-corner office.

I round the corner and see him sitting behind his desk like a five-star general. At 60-something years old and tall with glasses and gray JFK-style hair, he has a classy confidence about him. But, even though he smiles a lot in the hallways, you just know not to cross him.

"Take a seat," he says, motioning to the brown leather-studded chair.

There is no smile to be found on his face as I creep to the sophisticated execution chair.

His eyes meet mine and lock on. "Do you know why I called you in?"

"No, sir," I respond, sitting down.

Putting his elbows on his desk, he presses his fingertips together like a steeple. "Are you running for class president?"

"Yes, sir."

"Are you aware of our policy about campaign posters?"

"Um... no, sir," I say, timidly.

He reaches behind his chair and pulls out a white poster board that shows cut out magazine pictures of girl models in underwear. The poster reads: "We voted for Lawson... so should you!"

"I didn't make those!" I say in disbelief.

He pulls out another one that has a weed leaf and football helmet drawn on it, which reads: "I'll take a HIT for you!"

"Those aren't mine!"

"Is your name Lawson?"

"Yeah, but... Britney! I bet one of Britney's friends made those to set me up!"

Dr. Novak pulled out one more poster: "'Hey freshmen... let's 'break a leg' together."

Mr. Peters, are you referring to the Britney who got injured on the first day of school?

I feel my facing turning red.

"Yeah, I made that one, but she set me up on the others."

"You made a poster using her injury as a marketing ploy?"

"Well... yeah, but it was a joke."

"Mr. Peters, Britney will probably not be able to play the

sport she loves for the entire year, and her team will suffer for it. I do not find humor in that, nor do I find humor in any of these other posters."

"Yeah, but I didn't make those other posters."

"Can you prove that?"

I search frantically for an answer.

"Willow! Willow Harrison helped me make my posters last night, and she can tell you."

Dr. Novak picks up his phone and dials a number.

"Yes. Can you call Willow Harrison out of class, please? Thank you."

"Lawson, I'm going to call Willow into my office while you wait in the other room, so she doesn't know what this is all about. For your sake, I hope her testimony is favorable for you. Please, go sit in the chair in the room across the hall and close the door until I call you in."

I walk over to the room, close the door, and sit down.

I can't believe this. What will they do if they don't believe Willow? Suspend me? And, the game tonight! I'm panicking, and my hands feel clammy. They can't do this! There's no proof. Why don't they ask Britney and her friends about this? I try to calm myself with logic. Willow will testify for me, and they might make me redo the posters, but that's it. I'll be OK.

I hear Dr. Novak's voice across the hall.

"Sit down, Ms. Harrison."

I can't hear Willow's voice clearly. She is talking softly.

I feel like one of those people wrongly accused and sentenced to life in prison. Only five minutes have gone by, but it seems like twenty.

Knock, knock.

The door opens, and Dr. Novak is standing there, but Willow is nowhere in sight.

"Lawson, Willow supported your claim that you did not make those posters. However, you could have made them the night before or even this morning. So, at this point, you are not guilty, but I will need to do some further interviewing before making any decisions. Please wait here."

Over the course of 25 minutes, Dr. Novak talks to maybe three or four more people. One is Britney, because I can hear her disgusting, Golem-like voice.

Coach is going to kill me if I can't play tonight.

Knock, knock. The door opens, and Dr. Novak is standing there.

"Please come back in, Lawson."

He slowly walks behind his desk and sits down.

"Well, after several interviews, everyone is sticking to their stories. So, this is what we're going to do. You will have to make new posters, and anyone who hangs up posters from now on will need to have them approved."

"Yes, sir," I say, allowing myself to take my first breath in about 45 minutes.

"Thank you for coming in, and good luck with the elections. You're dismissed."

I leave before he can change his mind.

As I walk back into class, I see Britney and her friends smiling like little wretched demons. I stare back as I walk to my chair. I don't care. I want them to know that I wasn't afraid.

Willow reaches over and grabs my hand as I sit down.

I nod my head to let her know it was OK.

When class gets out, Willow and I walk to our lockers.

"Britney set me up with those posters, but I'm not in trouble. I just have to make new posters."

"Even the three-legged ones?"

"Yeah. Dr. Novak said they weren't funny."

"So, now what will we make?"

I think for a second. "Britney is a B—."

"Yeah. We can't do that."

"Bad person. I was going to say, 'Bad person.'"

"We can't do that, either."

How about "Snitches end up in ditches"?

"Yeah, that's much better." Willow is an expert at sarcasm.

"Hey, did you and Connor make up?" she asks hopefully.

I nod my head in a diagonal direction trying not to lie or tell the truth.

"Come on, babe," she says, pleading, "You two like each other."

I raise my eyebrows as if her statement is questionable. She shakes her head, turning away from me.

"Don't act like you're better than him," Willow warns.

"What? Why is everyone telling me what to do suddenly, as if I have to live how they tell me to?"

"Who is everyone?"

"Never mind," I say, trying not to go down that road. "Look, guys are sometimes different than girls, and they need more time to work things out. OK?"

She looks at me with skeptical eyes, like I am a kid telling my mom I'll do my homework later.

"So, you're good for your game tonight, right?" Willow asks, pointing to my throwing arm.

"Yeah," I say, shaking it out. "I can't believe I'm starting QB tonight."

"Isn't this what you always wanted?"

"Yeah... Yeah, it is," I say, feeling strange now that it's true and feeling nervous that I might mess it up.

"You'll do great," Willow says without hesitation... but also without much emotion.

I keep repeating Willow's words in my mind throughout the rest of the day, "You'll do great," because maybe I don't believe them.

―――――――

"Pregame, let's go!" Coach G yells as we exit the fieldhouse. Our cleats on the concrete sidewalk sound like a small army marching to the battlefield.

The stands are filling up. I mean, it's no varsity attendance turnout… but still. The student section is filling up, and parents dot the bleachers in anticipation to see the game. As I scan the bleachers, I see Mom and Dad seated next to Willow and her parents, near the top. Willow and I make eye contact, and she gives me a big wave.

The nerves in my stomach roll around with the mounting pressure. Sure, it's only a freshman game, but my whole high school career could hinge on how this game goes.

We take to the field and start our stretching and warm-ups. The other team is wearing green jerseys and gray pants while we wear our home white jerseys and silver pants.

Finally, I get to take some snaps and warm up my arm, which kind of feels like Jell-O. It's almost as if the stares from the crowd are zapping all of my energy. I see Tony on the sidelines wearing his boot with his crutches resting on the ground. Even though he wouldn't admit it, I know he doesn't want us to win with me as QB.

"Lawson!" Coach calls me over. "How you feeling, son?"

"Good, sir!" I realize that in football you lie a lot.

"We're leaning on you tonight, son, and I know you can do it. We're going to start the game off with a couple of run plays and then see if we can catch them off guard with some passes."

"Yes, sir!"

"OK! Good! Let's do Wedge Right 42 Blast. Come on, let's kick some ass," he says, swatting my butt back onto the field.

We stand on the sidelines as the national anthem plays over the speakers. We aren't important enough to have an actual pep band. The sky is clear, and the sun is to our backs. A warm breeze sails by, lifting the flag for a moment.

I remember Coach Rider's words on the first day of practice: "There are things about this sport that make it all worth it. It's why young men want to do all those crazy things."

This is what he was talking about.

We are set to kick off. With varsity, the QB usually doesn't play defense, but this is freshman football. You have to earn your keep. Besides, we have Gabe as a backup. I look over to see him staring at the sky. Even though he wants to play, he would definitely run off the field if he had to take a snap.

"…and the home of the… brave!"

The crowd cheers as we strap on our helmets and take to the field.

We line up, waiting for the kickoff so we can hurdle ourselves down the field like cannon balls. Some people say football is dangerous… and they're right. I was on the far right side of the line where they put the fast players who hope to run around the action and tackle the return runner.

The whistle blows, signaling that we have the green light. The kicker holds one hand high in the air to signal 'get ready.'

"Pwat!" The sound of the kicker's foot on the ball is like a starting gun in a track meet. A wave of 14- and 15-year-old bodies fly down the field.

"Pop! Pop!"

I can hear the sound of pads hitting as players collide.

Right, left, I dodge opposing tacklers. The return runner catches the ball about 15 yards away from me at the 20-yard line. Cutting in, I make a straight line for my victim. I want to crush him so badly to make a statement—

"Pop!"

Someone or something just torpedoed me, sending me flying 5 yards like a rolling tumbleweed.

"Ugh!" That hurt. I slowly stumble back to my feet and see the man/child who hit me.

No way is that kid a freshman… as I watch the runner make it to the 40-yard line before going down.

I run back to my position, trying to shake off the train that hit me. They line up in an I-formation with both running backs lining up behind the quarterback.

"Hike!"

The handoff is to the fullback running right up the gut of the line. Breaking a tackle, he hit open field and is heading in my direction.

With feet chopping, I close in on him.

I keep repeating to myself, "Focus on the belt, on the belt."

He fakes a right, and I dive in on him as he goes left. I get a hand on his jersey and squeeze it as if it were a million dollars. I swing around and grab his ankle, tripping him up and taking him to the ground. Both teams' crowd applauds, because a 9-yard run is good for them, and preventing a touchdown is better for us.

They march down the field, completing 5 yards here and 8 yards there. Finally, we stick them at the 38, so they have to punt. Since I am the fastest, Coach wants me to return.

The ball is kicked low and short, bouncing out at the 23-yard line. It's our ball!

With every play, a substitution is made on our team, so that the new player can tell me what play the Coach wants.

"Wedge Right 42 Blast on two. Wedge Right 42 Blast on two. Ready?"

"Break!"

We line up on offense, and the center takes a four-point stance on the ball.

"Blue 42!" I call out slowly, as if I want time to slow down or maybe rapture to begin.

"Blue 42!

"Hike! Hik—"

The other team's tackle lurches forward on a false start, and the referee blows his whistle.

"Offsides, defense. Five-yard penalty. Repeat first down," the referee calls out.

Here we go again. Maybe they will commit offsides fourteen times, and we'll get a touchdown.

I call the same play and count.

"Blue 42!

"Hike! Hike!"

The snap is clean, and I turn to do the quick handoff.

"Pow!"

We both get smashed during the handoff, causing me to nearly fumble.

What? That was, like, 2 seconds! Who was blocking that guy? I slowly get back up.

Not a great start… but at least I didn't fumble.

A player rotates in to tell me the next play.

"H39 Toss on one."

This is a halfback toss. I guess Coach doesn't believe in our line tonight.

"H39 Toss on one. H39 Toss on one. Ready?"

"Break!"

We line up, and I look at the tackler who just smashed me.

What's in these guys' food?

"Blue 42! Blue 42! Hike!"

I turn, do a quick toss, and follow to block.

"Pop!" I block off one defender, and our halfback finds an opening.

Five yards, 10 yards, and brought down near the 50-yard line.

Something is telling me that Coach is getting ready to call a pass play.

"Pop Pass 90 Backside on one."

Yup. This is a play for both tight ends to run an out toward each sideline.

Here we go. "Pop Pass 90 Backside on one. Pop Pass 90 Backside on one. Ready?"

"Break!"

"Don't throw an interception. Don't throw an interception," I keep repeating in my head.

"Blue 42! Blue 42! Hike!"

I drop back five steps, trying to separate myself from attempted tackles. I look to my left, and the tight end isn't open. The line is collapsing, and I feel the crosshairs on my chest. I look to the right and the tight end is open, moving toward the sideline.

Planting my foot, I cock the ball back and throw it toward his outside shoulder.

It is a beautiful pass—perfect loft and speed.

As it spirals through the air, I can picture the catch and touchdown run. Willow is in the stands probably getting weak in the knees, and her father is giving me his blessing.

The tight end drops the ball.

"What?" I say out loud.

The whole audience groans, and the tight end slaps his helmet in anger.

I can't believe it! The drop took the air out of my sails, deflating my hope.

Having no choice, we punt and exchange possessions with the other team the entire quarter until they score a touchdown in the second quarter.

Half time.

As we jog to the locker room, we are sure to get a tongue lashing from Coach.

"Boys," Coach says in a low voice, "…part of me wants to scream my head off. Blocking? What da hell? Put your body on someone! Now… the other part of me wants to tell you… we still have two quarters to send these little, well, giant, green corn-eatin', leprechaun-lovin' boys back to where they came from. NOW, GO GET YA SOME!"

I got to say, our football coaches can speak.

We bolt out of the building. It is time to show them what the Jaguars are made of!

The third quarter is miserable. We don't score, and they score another seven points on us.

By the fourth quarter, I am feeling it. Tired.

Second and ten on their 40-yard line, and we are on defense.

I think about us losing this game. I think about my team wanting Tony back. I also think about Britney and her friends laughing at me. Suddenly, something snaps inside of me, and I lose it.

Gritting my teeth... "Hike!" their quarterback yells.

The QB drops by to pass, and I can see his wide receiver cutting in on a slant. I just know he is going to throw to him. Digging my feet in, I lower my head and sprint to where the runner and ball will meet. He is going to catch it as soon as I get to him.

"Agh!" I let out a yell and spear him with all I have.

I send him back in a whiplash, landing on his back, popping the ball lose. Without hesitation, I jump up and grab the ball. Turning up field, I see an opening. A player tries to tackle me, but I dodge left. Another player comes, and I spin right. With all I have, I sprint into the open field to the 40, the 30, the 20, the 10... touchdown!

The crowd erupts, jumping up and down. I see Willow and our parents going out of their minds.

"Yes!" I shout, trying to catch my breath.

Coach and the rest of the team jumps up and down on the sideline. My teammates catch up to me, slapping my helmet. Tony is only person not celebrating. As we catch eyes he looks away at the scoreboard. The score is 7 to 14. We're still losing.

We exchange possession twice. Finally, we have the ball with the clock ticking down. We slowly make our way downfield to their 25-yard line.

We are exhausted, but we are so close to tying the game.

It is third down. We run a sweep and get stuffed.

Fourth down and only time for one more play. They know we are going for it and suspect it will be a pass.

Coach calls a post route to the same receiver who dropped it in the first quarter.

I know I can throw that ball.

I call the play and look my team in the eyes, "Ready?"

"Break!"

"Come on, come on, come on," I plead.

"Blue 42! Blue 42! Hike!"

Seven-step drop.

My receiver runs straight to the cornerback before darting at a 45-degree angle toward the end zone.

He has a step on him with some room to throw.

Now or never.

I plant, cock, and let it fly.

It is a beautiful pass; perfect loft and speed.

While it spirals through the air, I can picture the catch and touchdown. Once again, Willow is in the stands probably getting weak in the knees, and her father is giving me his blessing.

The receiver reaches up, the audience freezes…

Touchdown!

The crowd erupts, and I see Coach jumping up and down. I can't believe it! The score is 13 to 14. We need the extra point just to tie. I see Coach talking to the substitute player who is about to come in.

Is he going to call what I think he's going to call?

My teammate runs over to me.

"Quarterback sneak."

A rush of anxiety flows through me. We're not going for the tie, we're going for the win, and I'm the person who needs to run it in!

If I fumble, we lose.

If I don't make it to the end zone, we lose.

If I pee in my pants and pass out, we lose.

"Blue 42! Blue 42! Hike!"

Like a wave, our entire front line barrels forward as I push from behind, carrying the ball. With pads and helmets colliding and people grunting, we lunge forward and then get smashed to a halt. I can tell we aren't in the end zone yet, so I roll to the side looking for an opening.

I see the goal line, and the linebacker sees me.

I take two steps and lunge for the end zone while holding the ball out as the linebacker lunges for me.

Pop! He hits me hard and straight to the ground.

The ball slips out of my hands, rolling away.

"Fumble!" a player yells as others jump on the ball.

No! I lost the game!

The crowd is cheering, and all I can picture is our fans hanging their heads.

Suddenly, a player picks me up. It's Ethan. He's going to kill me. He is shouting in my face.

"Wooo! Wooo!"

What?

I look at the referee who has both hands straight up in the air.

The ball must have crossed the goal line! The two-point conversion is good!

"Final score: Jaguars 15, Fighting Irish 14. Jaguars win!"

The crowd is still cheering, and I see my parents.

I see Willow's parents.

I see Willow.

The lights…

The crowd…

The glory.

Chapter 12

"Stop clicking your pen like you're nervous. It's not like you're going to win!" Ethan teases me across the room, making everyone laugh.

It's the last period of the day, and they're about to announce the class election results for the freshman class. Britney isn't in this class, thank goodness. She would probably make me kiss her ring or something, if she won. I catch a glance from Tony, who is sitting next to Ethan. Unlike Ethan's teasing, I think Tony doesn't want me to win. When I got here, Tony was one of the most popular guys, and although he still is, so am I.

2:45 pm.

School is out at 2:50 pm. Did they forget? Is it a tie?

"Please excuse the interruption," the intercom blares. It is Mr. Bogart, the student council adviser.

Finally.

"We have the results for the freshman class elections."

I continue heaping clicking abuse upon my pen.

"There will be a short student council meeting right after school in room 120. All STUCO members are to attend.

First, we will announce the results for Treasurer."

Oh, *come on*! I can't take the suspense.

"Theresa Murray. Congratulations."

A few girls clap behind me.

"Now, for Secretary. Joyce White. Congratulations."

No one cares nearly as much as I do about this. I set the pen down and lean back in my chair, trying not to seem like my complete self-worth rests on the election results. How should I act if I lose? I didn't think this through…

"Vice President. Lance Bettis. Congratulations."

I can't let it show that I'm sad if I lose. I just need to smile and be confident like it doesn't matter.

"And, your freshman class president is…"

I can feel eyes on me.

Please.

"Lawson Peters. Congratula—"

The room erupts in applause. I won? I won! People slap my back and head, and then Ethan appears at the front of the room, holding a pen high in the air.

"To Lawson!" He yells like he is giving a toast and then starts clicking his pen frantically. People follow by clicking their pens. Ethan is dancing through the aisles like a maniac. Everyone is happy for me, everybody but one person: Tony, who is scrolling on his phone.

Oh, well. Let him be that way. I don't need him.

The bell rings, and we file out of class with people patting my back and calling me "Prez." Maybe Britney will congratulate me. That, or punch me. More students come up to congratulate me. I've never felt this liked before. It's an amazing feeling. If only my old friends and Emory could see me now. I went from a big fish in a small pond to a bigger fish in a bigger pond.

Sydney spots me from across the hall. "Lawson! Woohoo! Aww, I'm so proud of my little freshman." She wraps her touchy hands around me just as Willow rounds the corner. Willow's big loyal smile wilts as Sydney gives me a very friendly kiss on the cheek. Sydney catches my eye and looks over her shoulder to see my girlfriend in shock.

"Willow, right? You're Lawson's girlfriend!" Apparently, Sydney wasn't aware that kissing someone's boyfriend on the cheek isn't the best first impression.

Willow has her arms crossed and doesn't acknowledge Sydney. She nods her head as she stares at me like my personal pretty Terminator.

Sydney gets the hint and raises her shoulders and eyebrows while making a face to me that says, 'Whoops. Good luck with that.'

As Sydney leaves, I make a face to Willow like I was the one sexually harassed!

Willow's congratulation speech apparently got cancelled. "Please don't let another girl kiss you on the cheek," she says boldly with a dose of anger, her lips narrowing and eyes glaring.

"Willow! She just came up and did it!" I protest.

"So, tell her that she can't do that. Obviously, she knows you like it."

Willow waits for an apology.

"…Congratulations, Lawson. Yay! Happy moment…" I offer the words for her to say.

"Congratulations, Lawson," she says, hugging me like a mother hugs her hopeless, rebellious teenager.

"Come on, Lawson," Char says, passing us in the hall. "The STUCO meeting will start soon!"

"OK!" I reply, feeling like I've just been picked for the A-Team.

Willow forces a smile, but it falls flat. Her eyes, this time, are less angry and more hurt.

"Talk to you later. Are you going to the game?"

"No," Willow says, squeezing my hand. "I have relatives coming over tonight.

I give her another hug. "OK, well, I'll talk to you later, babe."

"Love you," she says, expecting me to say the same.

I don't like those kinds of *I love you's*. They feel like a test, like the only reason they're said is to see if the other person will say it back.

"Love you," I say, complying.

I let go of Willow's hand and make my way to room 120,

but just before turning down the hallway to the meeting, I bump into Liam, the junior from the party, coming out of the restroom.

"Laws," he says, messing with his phone and peering around as if looking for someone. "Hey, we're gonna go out tonight and find something to do if you wanna join."

"OK. Yeah." I say, acting like this isn't the first time an upperclassman wants me to hang out.

"OK. How about I pick you up after the varsity game?"

"Cool."

He dabs as he turns away. People wave and welcome me as I walk in the room. I feel like I joined a secret society of popular people.

"Welcome everyone! Take a seat," Char says from the front of the room. "Congrats to our newest freshmen members."

I look and see Theresa, Joyce, and Lance smiling like I am.

Char continues. "This is student council, where we represent our peers, coordinate events, and bring about changes they want to see."

Char seems way more mature than a 17-year-old.

"Alec, do you want to lead everyone in homecoming theme ideas?" Char says, gesturing to a senior.

"Hey, freshmen. I'm Alec, the senior class president." Alec is a clean-cut guy who might be Asian. He's tall and lean, wearing khakis and a polo. He walks to the dry-erase board.

"Let's start off with some theme ideas for homecoming."

A sophomore girl next to me raises her hand. "Vegas!"

"Okay. Good. Who else?" Alec asks.

"90's!" a guy yells from the back as the class laughs.

"Lawson," Alec says, zeroing in on me. "What do you think the freshman class would like?"

"Driver's licenses."

The class laughs harder.

"I'm kidding," I say, smiling. "I'm not sure."

"Come on, Lawson. Give us an idea," Alec insists.

"Umm… well, we are the Jaguars, so maybe something like a 'sophisticated safari?' I don't know. That's kind of dumb."

"No, no. That's good. Thanks for your input." Alec turns his attention to the rest of the group and asks for more input.

I settle back into my seat, shaking my head. I went from a nobody in this school to the class president!

Dope.

———————————

Boom! Boom! Boom! The bass drums thunder across the stadium, and the rest of the percussion follows, *rat, tat, tat, tat, tat!*

It's game time. Varsity football home game. The freshman football team doesn't have to attend the varsity games unless they're assigned to water boy. But JV does, and they have to suit up on the sidelines. I guess I caught the Coach's eye, because he's been having me suit up for JV as a backup along with Tony, Ethan, and a couple other guys.

"Go! Fight! Win!"

Our varsity cheerleaders are so hot.

We're playing the reigning district champ Wildcats, and we'll probably get crushed. Our varsity team is good—but not that good.

Sure enough, the first quarter immediately dropped us behind with 0 to 14. The rest of the game wasn't much better, with a final score of 10 to 42. I didn't get to play, which I'm thankful for, because it wouldn't have been pretty.

I change clothes, spray on some cologne, and head for the parking lot to wait for Liam.

My phone rings.

Willow.

"Hey, babe," I say, adjusting my bag on my back.

"Hey, Mr. President! Sorry that I couldn't come to the game tonight. My relatives are here now."

"It's OK. I didn't play."

"I miss you…"

"Yeah. Me, too. Hey, I gotta go, because I'm gonna hang out with Liam right now, and he's waiting for me."

"Really?" she asks, surprised.

"Yeah. Why?"

"Be careful, Lawson. You know he's no good."

"No good?" I ask, annoyed.

"Yes, and he's going to get you into trouble."

"Well, let's not be each other's parents. Okay?"

Silence. I've learned that silence is Willow's way of saying she disagrees.

"Hey, we can hang out tomorrow or something. Okay?" I can see Liam sitting in his car, looking at me.

"Lawson, that hurts when you think I'm trying to be your mom. I just—"

"Willow! It's okay, I'm not trying to fight or anything. Hey, I'll talk to you tomorrow. Okay?"

Silence again.

"OK?" I repeat.

"Bye," she says, hanging up quickly.

Man! Nag, nag, nag! She should be glad that I'm not some dork like Connor. Maybe she's religious and anti-anything-fun.

Tony and Ethan come up behind me. "What are you guys doing tonight?" I ask, slowing my pace.

"Relatives," Ethan says, checking his phone.

"You too! Willow has relatives in also."

I look at Tony and can literally taste the disdain he has for me. He is completely ignoring me.

"What's your problem, Tony?" I say, stopping right in front of him.

Tony tries to walk around me, but I don't let him.

"Why are you being an ass to me? Are you jealous that I'm

class president?"

"Are you serious?" He tries brushing me off again.

"Or, is it that I took your position?" I say, trying to pick a fight.

Tony stops dead in his tracks, locking eyes with me.

"Whoa…" Ethan says. "I'll let you two girls talk it out alone."

"Or, maybe you wish you had my girlfriend," I say, trying to dig in even deeper.

"F--- you!" Tony pushes me back.

"Is that your problem, huh?" I don't let up.

"Don't f--- with me, Lawson!" Tony says, getting in my face. "I don't give a sh-- about your prude girlfriend."

I want to punch him in his face, or maybe take a bat to his other ankle, and he knows it.

"Good choice," he says, referring to me not fighting. Tony is right. He could probably kick my ass, but I all need is one good blow to the back of his head. With nothing left to say, Tony passes me and heads to his car.

Liam is on his phone when I walk up to his parked black Dodge Charger and throw my bag on the back seat. Down the street we go with the windows down and some EDM music playing, as he talks on the phone with his elbow hanging out the window.

"Hey!" he says, finally hanging up and looking me, "Duuude, what's up?" He must not have seen me and Tony's face-off.

"I need a drink."

"Hell yeah! My man!" He says, pulling out a bottle from under his seat.

"What is this?" I ask, taking the clear bottle with tiny flakes floating inside.

"Goldschlager Schnapps. Those are actual real flakes of gold in there."

"What? Is it expensive?"

"Ha, not really, but it's freakin' cool! Well, go on! Dig for some gold!"

I took a big swig and immediately coughed as the burning alcohol coated my throat.

"Ha ha ha! You better not do that coughing around anyone tonight, you little puss!"

"Where are we going?" I ask, still watching the floating gold flakes.

"We're meeting up with some amigos at the North East Elementary playground."

"Elementary playground?"

"Yeah, the playground behind the school. Ha ha. It will be lit! I know it sounds dumb... but *it's not!*" Liam leans over and makes a crazy face.

We enter the front elementary school parking lot and drive around back where three other cars are parked near the basketball hoops. The playground is mostly dark, catching only part of the light that reflects from the parking lot.

"You babysitting, Liam?" a short stocky guy asks Liam as we get out of the car.

"Yeah, we need to train them young."

"Hey, I'm Laws—"

"I know who you are," he says, cutting me off. "Hey, I'm playing with you, man. I'm Nate."

"Yeehaaaaw!"

I look over Nate's shoulder and see several people playing on those animals you sit on that rock back and forth.

Man, this is a legit playground.

"Time to ride the bull, bro!" Liam tells me as we make our way over to the playground.

A girl is riding with one hand in the hair of what looked like a frog.

"OK, OK, let me show you how it's done, darling," Nate says, taking over the frog. She passes him a bottle of Jack Daniel's Whiskey.

"First, you take a shot, or two, of Jack," Liam instructs me as Nate takes a swig. "Then, we spin you around that spinning thing right there."

Nate gets on the merry go round, and everyone spins him around, like, twenty times.

"…then, you ride the bull."

"It's a frog," I say.

"Hahaha," Liam bursts out into laughter. "No sh--,

Sherlock! Bull… frog. Bullfrog!

Nate stumbles onto the bullfrog.

"Wooooo! Woooo! Yeehaw!" He rides the frog, bending it completely backward to where his back nearly touches the ground and then forward until falling off laughing.

I smell something funny.

Weed.

I turn around to see Liam smoking a joint.

"Laws, hit this, man."

"I don't smoke."

"You do tonight. Come on… just a little. You need to lighten up, man. You act too much like a freshman."

I take the joint and brought it to my lips.

I guess a little puff won't hurt.

I inhale a little and immediately coughed. I tried another puff, and this time, a little deeper.

"Yessir! OK, puff and pass, bro. Puff and pass." Liam says, pointing to the girls.

I walk over and hand the joint to one of the girls, and that's when I feel it. I've never been high before. It's a sensation that washes through your brain and body. It feels good.

Five minutes later, everyone is laughing. I'm laughing my head off, too, as we puff and pass the joint.

Headlights appear from around the corner.

"Sh--! Is that a cop?" Nate asks, freaking out.

Everyone gets up and starts moving backward.

"Chill, everyone," Liam says, "It's friends."

Three girls and a guy get out of a white Explorer.

Sydney? Is that Sydney from Biology?

She is holding hands with another girl. They come over and start talking to Liam, and then Sydney spots me.

"There's my hot freshman!" she yells, running over to me. "So, you're one of us after all. Huh?"

She puts her arms around me and spins me around.

"Ha ha," I say. "I guess so."

"And you smell amazing," she says breathing me in.

I can't think of what she is talking about since I just came from a football game until I realize it's the weed.

"Come meet my girlfriend," she says, taking me by the hand.

"This is Chloe." She grabs the slender arm of a tall tanned girl with straight black hair and dark green eyes.

Even though she doesn't have any makeup on, she is naturally gorgeous. Just the way she moves is seductive. "Hey, darling," Chloe says to me leaning in. Her breath is warm, and her touch is seductive. She kisses my cheek, and I briefly notice a tattoo on her neck but can't make it out.

She is very pretty, and like Sydney, very flirty.

We spend the next hour hanging out, drinking, and joking. I end up in one of the slide tunnels with Sydney and Chloe.

"Do you have chest hair?" Chloe teases me.

"Stop, Chloe," Sydney says, laughing. "It's not like he's 11 years old."

"OK, well, do you have a girlfriend?" Chloe asks, scooting closer to me.

"Uh, yes," I grin. "Her name is Willow."

"Freshman?" she asks.

"Yeah."

"Does she ever do this to you?" Chloe leans in and slowly starts kissing my neck.

My body retracts from the unexcepted wet sensation on the right side of my next. "Uh, no, not yet," I say, not sure what to do.

"Or this?" Sydney grabs the hair on the back of my head and starts making out with me while Chloe continues making circles with her tongue on my neck.

Sydney's warm mouth sucks on my bottom lip while Chloe slowly glides her tongue up my neck just beneath my ear. My body starts to tense up before giving way to what it wants. Chloe softly bites my earlobe and pulls my head back by my hair. Sydney's tongue slips in a little, and I hear myself breathing heavier.

I know I'm cheating, and I know it's wrong. But, I don't stop. I want more. I reach out my hands to touch them, but they both pull away laughing.

"Too bad you have a girlfriend," Chloe says, leaning back.

"Yeah. Well, we can keep going if you are single... So, are

you single yet?"

"Well…" I say, not thinking straight and drunk with lust.

I feel something on my leg and look down to see Sydney's hand stroking and squeezing my thigh.

"Well, I guess…"

Crash! The sound of breaking glass makes us all jump.

"Geez, man!" Nate says from outside. We climb out of the tunnel and see a large hole in the glass window on the side of the school. "Dude, I was trying to hit you with the rock, not the window!" They both laugh as they inspect the shattered window on the back side of the building.

The rest of us go over to the shattered window and peer inside the classroom.

"Hey, does anyone need a tablet? There are about fifteen of them in here." Nate asks.

Nate starts carefully crawling through an opening in the window.

"What are you doing, Nate?" Sydney asks.

"Getting a tablet," he says, smiling like a bandit.

"Get me one too, man," Liam says.

Other people start chiming in.

"Me, too!"

"Me, too!"

Nate grabs the whole stack and passes them to Liam.

"Aren't you guys scared about getting caught?" I finally ask.

Everyone stops and looks at Nate and Liam.

"Are you scared of getting caught?" Nate says, mocking me. "So, don't get caught, stupid."

The confliction inside my conscious stirs again. It bangs on the door like a friend's last attempt to save the person he once knew. Drinking is one thing, and then weed, and even kissing other girls, but this is stealing! I have to get out of here, but the marijuana is flowing through my blood like a kid in a bouncy house. Damnit. I'm so stoned.

"Well," Liam says, looking around. "On that note, let's get out of here."

We all pile into our vehicles and take off like criminals, because, well, we are. I have a sick feeling in my stomach, but it doesn't seem to bother anyone else as they mess with their tablets.

Liam pulls up to my house and drops me off first, since I have a midnight curfew.

"No tablet?" Liam asks through the window as I get out.

"No, man, you can have it."

Liam examines my eyes like he's searching for any lack of loyalty and the chance that I might snitch. "OK, but Laws... It goes without saying that your mouth stays shut on this. It's for all of our good, including yours." Liam's voice had taken on a tone I never heard from him before. His eyes flicker with shades of darkness.

"OK," I say, slowly backing away from the car. Liam

grins like he just sniffed out the phony in the group who doesn't belong, the imposter who doesn't want to stay but who knows too much to be able to leave.

His black charger slowly backs out of my driveway before taking off down the dark street.

I reach inside my bag and spray on some more cologne. My hands shake slightly. My nerves. I'm scared. To be sure, I smell different parts of my body for weed; my arms, my legs, my fingers... my fingers are the worst from holding the joint. A spray right on my fingers will fix that. The cool spray covers my entire hand erasing evidence like washing off blood from the murder weapon.

But, I didn't take a tablet, and I didn't break the window. I'm okay... right? I want to believe that, but something inside tells me I'm not.

Chapter 13

"Gravy?" Mom asks, holding the bowl in front of me, shaking me out of my thoughts about last night. The evening news is on as we sit at the kitchen island.

"You okay, sweetie?" Mom asks me, even though I know it's the question I should be asking her. Her smile is weak and glossy, like a mannequin in a fading outlet store.

"Yeah, Mom. Thanks."

Dad is also quiet. I can tell something is bothering him, but I guess, like all of us, he doesn't want to talk about it.

"*...North East Elementary School officials reported vandalism and theft last night as a window was smashed in and twelve tablets were stolen...*"

I quickly turn my head to the TV and see footage of the broken window and playground.

The reporter is standing right where I was standing less than twenty-four hours ago. "*Police say they are looking for anyone who may have leads on this case.*"

"That makes me sick!" Dad exclaims. "What kind of thugs would vandalize an elementary school? This country is going to crap. I'll tell you what needs to be done," Dad continues, growing angrier. "They need to find out who did that and put their butts in jail and let the other inmates teach them a lesson!"

"That is horrible," Mom says, still looking at the TV.

"Lawson, do you know anything about this?" Dad asks, ready to arrest someone himself.

I know I need a quick response to not sound suspicious. "No, I don't, but that's crazy."

I continue eating, acting like it doesn't bother me.

What if I confessed everything? I didn't break the glass or steal the tablets, so Dad wouldn't whoop me that hard, but he would report Liam and everyone else, and that would put me on their hit list. So much for being the popular kid; I would be bullied. Then again, if he ever discovered I was lying, he would put me in jail himself.

For the first time, I felt I could be in some serious trouble. I mean, the posters in Dr. Novak's office were one thing, but this is juvenile detention stuff!

The table is quiet again.

Silverware clanks on white porcelain plates. Big bites—chew, chew, chew. I want to escape to my room.

Done.

"Good dinner, Mom. I'm going upstairs to do some homework," I say, hopping out of my chair and heading for the stairs.

"Lawson," Dad says suddenly.

It was a tone that I couldn't escape from, and I know whatever Dad is about to say isn't going to be a surprise announcement that we're going to Disney World. Dad wipes his mouth, takes a deep breath, and puts his elbows on the table with folded hands.

Does he already know that I was out with Liam; did somebody tell him? I swallow hard.

Mom sits still, giving no cues as to what Dad is about to say.

He stares ahead as if he doesn't want to speak.

"I—" Dad pauses, looking out the window. "...I lost my job today."

Mom covers her mouth with her hands.

"They let me go—"

"Why?" Mom asks through her hands.

"A while ago, Tony installed the wrong part on the assembly line, causing a big mess and a lot of waste. We got behind and couldn't catch up. Then—" Dad's voice raises with his hand gestures. "Then one of our main machines broke down, so I shifted production onto the other machine and doubled production, but we had a huge bottleneck, which slowed us down even further. So, my boss came in and started degrading me and wouldn't stop on how 'incompetent' we all are... and I lost it."

"What do you mean?" Mom asks.

Dad's eyes fill with anger and remorse.

"I yelled back. I said that it wasn't my fault and that I didn't deserve this treatment."

Dad sighs and lowers his head. "So... he told me, 'You're right. You deserve worse. You're fired!'"

I slowly move back toward the table.

"Damnit!" Dad bangs the table with his fist, startling me and Mom.

"It's okay, Doug," Mom says, trying to console him. "You'll find another job."

"Another job?" Dad yells. He turns toward her. "I'll be blacklisted at all the other plants! This was my one shot, and it's gone!"

"We'll find another way, Doug." Mom's voice is trembling and nearly pleading at this point.

Dad bangs his fist on the table again. "How am I going to pay for this house? And, you..." he says to Mom. "You can't work either!"

Mom covers her face with her hands and starts crying.

Dad stands, and rubbing the back of his neck, he walks to the window.

"I'm sorry, everyone. It's all my fault..." He trails off as he walks out of the room.

I stand there feeling helpless, watching Mom cry.

I gently rub her back. I have never seen Mom like this. Insecurity and fear overwhelms me.

"I'm sorry... I'm sorry," she keeps muttering between

sobs.

I feel like the parent trying to console the child. "It's not your fault that you're depressed," I say, trying to lift her spirits.

Just hearing the word 'depressed' makes her cry harder.

Anger swells up in my chest toward Dad. Why isn't he consoling Mom? He's so selfish!

Mom pats my hand and grabs a tissue to wipe her eyes, "Thank you, sweetie. It will be okay." She gets up and leaves the room—I'm assuming—to look for Dad.

She puts herself last, which I don't see as noble. I see it as weak.

My phone rings. It's Willow.

"Hey," I say, picking it up.

"Lawson, do you know anything about what happened at North East Elementary school last night?"

I don't have the guts to tell her since she did give me the speech about how Liam would only get me into trouble. I also don't have the guts to tell her that I made out with two sophomore girls in the tunnel of a playground slide. No matter how I try to justify it, I cheated. It's funny how black and white things are in your moral conscious until you're the guilty one.

I don't think of myself as a bad person, but what I did was wrong, so was it a mistake? I wouldn't do it again, so it's okay, right? I mean, I learned my lesson.

"No. I don't know anything." I say somewhat convincingly.

"Why did someone tell me that you made out with two sophomore girls the other night, Lawson?"

"What?" I am caught off guard and need time to think.

"Tell me, Lawson." Her voice is stern.

"No. No! They're making it up to get me into trouble. Do you think I would do that?"

I am totally committed now, and there is no turning back. I know I lied, but I am sticking to it. I messed up, but I'm not going to let it ruin our relationship!

"Don't lie to me," she says, softly.

"I'm not!"

A few seconds of silence go by, and then a message pops up on my phone. It's a picture text.

I open it and am horrified to see a picture of myself, Sydney, and Chloe sitting inside the slide tunnel... making out. It was taken from far away, but you can still see...

Who took this? Who took this? Liam? Nate? *Who took this?*

"Bye, Lawson."

"Wait! I'm sorry. *Willow*! Don't hang up. Please, I'm sorry. I didn't mean it. They don't mean anything to me! They came onto *me*!"

"I don't care, Lawson."

"Well, what do you want from me, Willow? I said I am sorry! Come on, what do you want me to say?"

A brief pause on the other end of the phone made me want to come out of my skin, or perhaps, retreat deeper into it.

"Remember what I said at Brad's house when he asked me, 'What do I want?'"

I frantically try to remember her words.

"I said that I wanted people to be less fake."

"So, you're saying I'm fake?" I snap back, trying not to concede defeat.

Willow maintains her composure. "I'm saying I have a way of seeing the best in people and falling in love with their potential, but then getting let down by the reality of who they are."

"So, that's the only reason you went out with me? To fix me? Who else have you tried fixing? Tony?"

"You were a different person last summer back when... back when you cared about more than being popular... Bye, Lawson."

I hate my life.

I want to leave. I... I just want to go! I storm out the front door and run as fast as I can down the sidewalk. I want to go as far away as possible and get away from everything. Rage overtakes me, and I want to hit something, kill something! The breeze whips across my face like lashings of punishment. I run faster. *Faster! Why is everything falling apart?*

Suddenly, something jumps in front of me from the

bushes next to the sidewalk, causing me to fall over.

It's a deer—a fawn with its spots barely visible.

Stopping about twenty feet away, it turns and stares at me. Our eyes lock in fear, and our hearts beat in unison. It's still, waiting for me to move.

The fawn is so beautiful. I've seen deer before and even went deer hunting, but something was different this time. This time… I can relate to it.

Maybe it's lost or its parents have died. Either way, it's as if it doesn't know what to do or where to go. Slowly, it crosses the street while keeping an eye on me and then trots past some houses into Brad's yard.

Brad.

What time is it? It's not too late, right? I need to talk to Brad!

I run over and knock on his door. It opens, and Brad looks surprised to see me.

"Lawson," he says. "You okay?"

I don't have to say anything.

"No, you're not. Come inside."

We go into his office and sit down.

"What happened, Lawson?"

I look at the floor, not knowing where to begin and reluctant to tell Brad everything. My chest heaves up and down still trying to catch its breath.

"Lawson?"

I look up.

"Whatever it is, you can tell me, son."

The word 'son' touches me. I know he means it as a figure of speech, but it feels like more.

Taking a deep breath, I shake my head.

"I screwed up."

"Tell me everything."

"Willow broke up with me, I might be in trouble with the law, and my family is falling apart."

"Start from the beginning. Tell me everything."

"A junior at school named Liam asked me to go out with his friends to party at North East Elementary School."

Brad leans back in his chair and clasps his hands together. He must have seen the evening news based on his worried look.

"I didn't have anything to do with breaking the glass or stealing tablets! I swear! I didn't even take one, but I did make out with two girls, and someone somehow got a picture of it and sent it to Willow. I didn't know about the picture, so I lied at first. I also lied to my parents about not knowing anything about the North East Elementary School incident. Plus, I found out tonight that my dad was fired, and he doesn't know if we can afford the house! Mom has anxiety and depression and can't work..."

I feel a lump in my throat, and my lip starts to quiver. I struggle to speak clearly without crying.

"If I tell anyone about the vandalism, Liam will probably hurt me."

The lump grows. I cough, trying to strengthen my voice.

"I don't know what to do, and I feel--"

"Alone." Brad leans forward, resting his elbows on the desk while folding his hands beneath his chin. He furrows his eyebrows in deep thought and looks at me.

"You're scared."

I nod my head, and my eyes start to water.

"That's why you lied to Willow and your family."

I keep nodding.

"Are you angry?"

"Yes," I say softly.

"Who are you angry with?"

"At whoever took that picture, at Liam for breaking the window and stealing the tablets, at Dad for losing his job—"

"Are you mad at Willow?" he asks, cutting me off.

"No."

"Why?"

"Because it's not her fault."

"Whose fault is it?"

I look away, because I know what he wants me to say.

"It's partly my fault."

"Partly?"

"Yeah, they just came onto to me."

"But you went to the party and--"

"So, I can't go to parties anymore?" I ask defensively.

"No, you can! You can do whatever you want, Lawson!" Brad yells, standing up. "You can go to parties, you can drink, you can make out with girls, you can lie, and you can run! And where has it all gotten you?"

I don't answer. I can't.

He walks to the window and looks out.

"You know the saying that 'all actions have their consequences whether good or bad?' It sounds like something adults say. So, let me say it differently..."

He walks over to his easel and flips through the chart pages until stopping on one.

"Remember this page? You asked me one day what 'face the enemy' meant. Well, I'll tell you what it means. When my wife and daughter died..."

He starts choking up and walks away from the flip chart.

"When my wife and child died, I died." He looks away as if trying to regain his composure and then looks back at me.

"My laughter died. My patience died. My creativity died. My world died. And, I felt empty, and then that emptiness got filled with hatred; hatred toward God and the driver who hit them. But, your body can't stay mad forever, so it breaks down and cries. Sadness doesn't describe how I felt. So, after I cried, I got mad, and after I got mad, I cried. I felt like my soul was purging itself, but eventually I felt numb to the emotions, because I had felt them for so long that they became old. My heart became as hard as a rock. I just... didn't... care. I wanted to die."

He starts pacing again, trying to keep it together.

"So, I researched 'how to commit suicide.' I chose an option, and I prepared myself. I was going to kill myself, Lawson. I was going to do it! But something happened. The night that I was going to do it, on the very night of..." He let out a big sigh. "My doorbell rang. I didn't want to answer it. I knew they would go away if I didn't. But, part of me didn't want them to—whoever it was. I don't know. Maybe part of me was hoping it was my daughter and somehow God brought her back..."

Brad walks over to the door and opens it.

"I opened the door, and it was a boy. He was nervous and scared. He handed me a flyer and said, 'Hi, my name is Connor, and I cut grass.'

"My yard was the worst in the neighborhood. I mean, it was bad... but the funny thing was, it saved me. Because, I stood there looking at Connor, and I saw myself. Scared. Unsure. Lonely. I was just like Connor when I was a kid. And, I felt something that I hadn't felt in years—meaning."

Brad closes the door and walks back to his desk.

"I saw my purpose. This kid, Connor, was lonely. I could tell because I knew what lonely looks like. I knew he needed me. I didn't care about my yard, but in that moment, I cared for Connor like he was my family... because I didn't have one."

He rubs his face, trying to shake the emotions.

"It wasn't my fault that my family died in a car crash. It wasn't my fault that I felt angry and sad. It wasn't my fault!" Brad slams his hand on the table. "But, if I gave up…THAT would have been my fault, because my enemy was no longer the driver or God… it was me. And, that day, I faced him."

Brad sat down in his chair.

"Your enemy, Lawson, is not Liam or Nate or your dad. You have a reason to be angry about those things, but your real enemy… is you. The body's natural reaction is to protect itself even if that means telling lies and running from the truth. The problem is that the body is like a scared animal that doesn't know when the running and hiding stops being helpful and starts being hurtful."

"Like a deer running into traffic," I say, startled by the coincidence.

"Exactly. Fear is normal, but even though fear is meant to protect, it can harm. It might save you at first, but it can kill you in the end. And the things we fear usually aren't the things we should fear. Your fear of losing Willow made you lie, which is the real reason you lost Willow. You should have been afraid of losing her trust, not her knowing the truth."

I wince from the truth of his words.

"But something that's lost can, sometimes, be found. Willow loves you, Lawson." Brad looks at me straight in the eyes. "She's angry, scared, and trying to protect herself. She also knows that if she lets you cheat on her, she would not be helping herself or you. If we love someone, we're willing to do something hurtful in order that it might become helpful.

"Yeah, I know," I respond, feeling guilt and remorse.

"It's easy to know, Lawson. The hard part is doing. By the way, if you see others as scared deer, like you said earlier, everyone's actions will start making a lot more sense."

"So, you're saying Liam is scared?"

"Absolutely. He's scared of getting caught, but more importantly, I think he's scared of looking scared. He's scared of uncertainty. The most popular kids usually are."

"Like me when I moved here."

"And, you found your certainty in popularity. Popularity is not bad, but seeking it makes it so. Lawson, you were willing to sacrifice your character for your security, but the paradox is that we can do what's wrong even when we know it's wrong—in order to try to feel right. If you want to feel right, do right, even if it doesn't feel good at first. It will in the end."

Brad sits up straight in his chair.

"So, what do you need to feel?" he asks.

"I need to feel sorry."

"No. You are sorry that you got caught, but that is not the right kind of sorry."

"Uh… I need to feel… I don't know… what?"

"Empathy."

He points his finger at me.

"When you can feel what someone else feels without being blinded by your own feelings, you are learning to love. You're a leader, Lawson, but I imagine that you haven't been leading well. It's been all about you, and that's easy to do. It's our instinct. Selfishness is fear's cousin, but leadership starts with love, and love starts with empathy. And, love has cousins also: responsibility and courage. You are responsible if you choose to respond with your ability to do so. You are able to do so, Lawson, but you are lacking courage."

"How do I become more courageous?"

"Courage comes from encouragement, which I'm trying to give you tonight, but I can't be courageous for you."

"So... how?"

"How did you throw that touchdown pass on fourth down?"

I look at him, confused. How does he know that?

"How did you run that quarterback sneak with the game on the line?"

"How do you know about that?" I ask.

"I was there."

"What?"

"I've been at every game."

"But... I... didn't see you! Why didn't you tell me?" I'm shocked and mad for him not telling me.

"You see what you look for. If you had been looking for me, you would have seen me."

He's right. I was so caught up with myself and Willow, I didn't even look.

"How did you do it, Lawson?" He looks at me and grins. "How did you win the game?"

"I don't know... I..."

"You practiced, and there was probably some luck, but how else?" he persists.

"I don't know."

"I'll tell you how," Brad leans forward, "...because you focused on winning more than on not losing. Courage is focusing on what needs to happen rather than on what might happen."

I look at Brad, and he looks at me.

"What needs to happen, Lawson?"

We don't break eye contact; he won't let me. My fears become so clear to me. I can see it. I can feel it, and now I can finally stop outside of it. I feel my fears shrinking, dying like they were being choked out by something bigger. Something starts swelling up inside of me. It isn't anger but something similar, something strong. He sees it in my eyes.

"You feel it?" he asks.

"Yes."

"What is it?"

"Courage."

"Call your parents and tell them you'll be home late."

"What? Why?"

"We have work to do. Call them now."

I pull out my phone but hesitate, wondering whether I should call Mom or Dad. I call Dad.

"Hey, Dad. I'm at Brad's house, the neighbor down the street—"

Brad motions for me to give him the phone.

"Mr. Peters, hi. I'm the guy your son cuts grass for. Yes. I agree. You have a fine son. Well, I want you to know that I'm giving him some free tutoring lessons, and he'll be home later. Okay. Yes. Bye."

"But, I didn't bring my books," I say, confused.

"We're not talking math, Lawson. We're talking leadership." Brad grins before darting into the kitchen and returning with a big growler of Kombucha.

"Ginger blend. You're in the big leagues now."

I take the glass he poured and take a sip.

"Man, that's strong!"

"That's what we're going for, cowboy. Okay!" Brad scurries over to his flipchart and starts ripping off the old pages.

"What's the purpose of a leader?"

"Um... to lead people—"

"Redundant. What does it mean to lead?"

"To... uh... show them the way—"

"What way?"

"The best way."

"Who decides that?"

"Uh…"

"Lawson, you're sounding more like a dictator than a leader," Brad says, smiling.

"A dictator is like a bully," Brad explains. "A bully certainly influences and gets people to do things, but it's the things he or she wants them to do. For those leaders, it's all about control. We don't want that. We want the good kind of leadership."

"Okay, so what is the good kind of leadership?" I ask.

Brad scribbles something on the easel.

"Empower?" I ask, confused.

"To empower means to create power inside someone else."

Brad leans over and turns off the light switch, darkening the room.

"Wh… what are you doing? I can't see."

"Hold on," Brad says, stumbling across the room, fumbling through a drawer.

A flame flickers as he holds a candle and lights it. With the lit candle in one hand, he walks over and hands me an unlit candle.

"Take it," he says. "Now, what's the purpose of my candle?" he asks.

"To light the room?"

"Yes!" he says enthusiastically, with his faced illuminated

by the flickering flame. "Now that my candle is lit, I have light, and I have power. So, what can I do with my light and power?"

"Um... light up the room?"

"I'm already doing that. What else can I do?"

"Uhh... create heat?"

"Ha ha, you're getting warmer."

He leans over to me while slowing moving his candle toward mine. His flame touches the tip of my candle wick, and slowly it catches my wick on fire. The two flames grow together, and then he pull his candle away. Mine is still lit.

"What can I do with my light and power?"

"Light mine," I say, smiling at my flame.

"I can empower you. My flame isn't any less because I empowered you. In fact, it was larger when our candles were together."

"Like *The Giving Tree*." This starts to make sense as I gaze at the flame.

"Lawson," Brad says, pulling my attention away from the flame. "Much is given, much is required. Be the light and light up others."

The shadows flicker and dance across the walls. I feel it in my heart: love, courage.

"OW!" Brad shouts, making me jump and nearly drop my candle.

"Hot wax!" he says, turning on the light and setting his

candle on his desk.

"So, the purpose of leadership is to empower others?" I ask.

"Yes, empower others to empower others to empower others—"

"Okay. I get it, but how do I do that?"

"Ahh," Brad says, slowly walking around the room while thinking.

"You do what you know is right... with what you know you can do... to help others with what they think they can't do."

"Whoa, say that again."

"You do what you know is right with what you know you can do to help others with what they think they can't do. So, what do you think is right?"

"Honesty," I reply.

"Keep going..."

"Loyalty, responsibility, integrity..."

"Keep going!" Brad says, scribbling on the flipchart.

"Trustworthiness, discipline, humility..."

"*Yes! Yes! Keep going!*"

"*Courage, faith, love!*" I shout back, like I am on a game show.

"Okay, okay. Do what you know is right with what you know you can do. So, Lawson, what CAN you do?"

"Umm... Umm... I can..."

"Yes! Right there. You can speak. You can use words, and what words?"

"Encouragement?"

"Yes. Give an example," Brad says, writing fiercely.

"Good job. Don't quit. You can do it…"

"Yes. What else?"

"Um… hold people accountable!"

"YES!" Brad writes the following on the flipchart: "Speak truth with love even if it's tough love. But don't speak truth until they first feel love."

"How?" I ask.

"People feel love in different ways. Some people like positive words, others like quality time, and still others like a pat on the back or even a hug. When in doubt, do all the above. Most importantly, make sure you do it with good motives. Don't treat them like a project. They'll feel manipulated."

"Wow! That's good," I say.

Brad does a little dance. "You're not done. Come on. One more! What can you do with your words?"

"Umm…"

"Come on. Tell me!"

"*Uhh…*"

"*Tell me!*"

"*I don't know!*"

Brad smiles and slowly writes something on the flipchart: "Admit when you don't know."

I laugh. "Why are you so premeditated with everything?"

"It's what I do." He grins like a mischievous kid. "Okay. Now, what's more powerful than your words?"

"Actions!"

"Boom! Actions speak louder than words. What can you do?"

"Ahh… this is hard."

"You're doing it right now."

"Thinking?"

"Okay. Yeah. That's one, but not the one I'm thinking of."

"I'm trying, but…"

"YES! Try. You can try. Even if you fail, you can try.

He writes 'try' on the paper.

"And even if you try and fail, you can what?"

"Retry?"

"Good… but what should you do before you retry?"

"Come on, Brad, you're killing me!"

"I'm teaching you, and I just gave you that one for free." He writes 'teach' further down the page.

"Before you can teach, you must what?"

"Learn," I said, finally getting it.

"To learn, you must what?" He pulls on his ear and coughs.

"Cough?"

He throws his arms in the air in defeat.

"I'm kidding!" I say. "Listen. I must listen."

He walks over to me and puts his fingers on my ears. "These are more important and powerful than this," he says, pointing to his mouth. "To not only understand another human being, but for them, feeling understood is more powerful than any speech you can give, because when you touch someone's heart, you can move their feet, and you do that more by listening than by speaking."

He walks back to his desk, sits down, and takes a sip of Kombucha.

"Ahh… Okay" I think I'm starting to get it. "So, you do what you know is right with what you know you can do to help others with what they think they can't do."

With his elbows resting on his desk, Brad taps his fingers together. "Who is that for you?"

"People who—"

"No, Lawson. Give me names."

"My mom, my dad…"

"Good. Who else?"

"…Connor."

"Good! Deeper."

"I can't think of anyone else."

"Darker."

I stare at the flipchart, realizing where he's taking me. "But," I hesitate. "But, they don't want me—"

"They're scared deer, Lawson."

I don't want to say their names.

"Who?"

I cringe, feeling afraid to let go of my anger and judgement on the names of those who have hurt me.

"WHO?"

"Tony, Liam, Britney."

"Lawson," Brad says. "A leader must help people by loving people, and to do that, they must forgive people, because resentment clouds your thinking and hardens your heart. And, you need to see what they can't see and feel what they are afraid to feel."

"But, but you said, 'to helps others with what they think they can't do.' So, what can't they do?"

"They can't see their own weaknesses and the need for humility. They also can't see happiness without popularity. Besides, you're not only helping people with what they can or can't do, Lawson. You're helping them with what they can become."

"How do I change them?"

Brad leans back and crosses his arms, "They have to see it. They have to see themselves clearly, and they have to want to change. Love is the best way. It has a way of cutting through fear and speaking to the heart."

"How?"

"Love is patient. Love is kind. It is not easily angered. It does not hold grudges. It never fails."

"But, what if they reject me? I fail, right?"

"Love is patient and it perseveres. You weren't ready to talk to me a few weeks ago, but here you are tonight. You can't make someone accept love, but if they reject you, you did not fail. Your flame still burns," he says, pointing to me and the flickering candle on his desk at the same time. "And, no one can put it out except for you, and that's the problem."

"What do you mean?"

"Lawson, when you start leading and loving, you will get rejected. Some people will even try to put your light out, because they're testing your sincerity. It's human nature. If you get mad and give up, they feel it proves that you never really loved them. And, worst of all, you'll start becoming like them. Fear wants to create more fear. Hate wants to create more hate. But, love... love wants to understand. Love wants to create more love.

"I struggle with being nice to someone who isn't nice to me. They don't deserve it."

"You're right. They don't, but... people who deserve love the least need it the most. And, by doing that, you're leading. You're influencing. You're being a role model."

"Have you forgiven the driver who hit your wife and kid?" The thought was blurted out without thinking. Brad quickly looks away, caught off guard by my question.

"Oh, I'm sorry—"

"No, it's okay. I..."

"Have you met with him and talked to him?"

Brad knows I am trying to flip his words on him. I can tell he doesn't want to answer my question. My questions were too personal. "I'm sorry, I just—"

Brad raises his hand in the air, silencing me. "I do know him and where he lives. He lives in jail about two hours from here. And, no… I haven't visited him."

I don't say anything else. I feel bad for bringing it up. I can only imagine how much anger he must have for him. "The student becomes the teacher," Brad says, composing himself and forming a smile.

We sip Kombucha in silence. I guess we both have a lot to think about.

The flame flickers on the dark wooden desk—a soft yellow glow above a white candle.

Chapter 14

Homecoming week.

Each day has a different theme this week. Pajama Day, Sports Team Day, Twin Day, Superhero Day, and Class Color Day. So, I'm walking into school with my pajamas—well, not really... I wear boxers to bed, but that's not allowed in school, so I have some flannel pants on that my grandma gave me last Christmas. I step into human geography class with Mr. Wright, and Willow pretends not to see me as she doodles on her paper.

I think we're broken up, but I'm not sure. I mean, she said, 'Bye Lawson,' on the phone, which could just mean that she's hanging up, but it definitely sounded more permanent. I slip into my seat not knowing whether to look at her or not. Do I still love her? Yes. Was I wrong? Definitely. I made out with two girls in an elementary school playground! Yeah, that was wrong. I feel terrible, but I don't even know how to make it up to her. It's like I shouldn't be given the opportunity.

As Mr. Wright begins class, I find it hard listening. Will it be this awkward between us for the rest of the year? I have to do something. I start writing a note. What do I say? 'I'm sorry?' Frustrated by my incompetence as a human being, I feel like shoving the pen in my heart. OK, maybe that's a little dramatic. I could flip over my desk and start crying my eyes out in a plea for forgiveness. Yeah, that could work. I have no idea what Mr. Wright is talking about. Maybe I'll flunk out of this class and then slowly spiral down to where I'm kicked out of school but still mope around outside like a beggar trying to get Willow to take me back. I mean, it's possible.

I find myself now doodling on the paper. What would Brad do? It's kind of like 'What would Jesus do?' Well, he said to be straight forward and gentle, but that was when I was doing the breaking up. Now, I'm doing the unbreaking up. I decide to write something. My pen moves slowly across the paper. 'Sorry for what I did. There's no excuse. I don't expect you to forgive me.'

I slide the note over and look to the front of the room, hoping she will acknowledge my apology, but she doesn't. It sits there, and sits there, and sits there. I know the other two students at our table see it. They must be thinking this is so awkward, and I'm a complete loser.

Class is over, and Willow gets up, leaving her untouched note on the desk. I wait for her to leave, and then I shove the note in my pocket. Brad said people would test my sincerity.

"Laws." It's Liam walking up to me in the hallway like

The Godfather. He knows I didn't approve of them stealing the tablets, and maybe he doesn't trust that I will keep my mouth shut. Before Liam reaches me, Tony swings around the corner. He looks at me and then Liam.

"Oh, hey, Liam," Tony says with a big grin. "Why are you hanging out with Lawson? He talks sh—on you behind your back."

Liam glares at me.

"He's lying," I say without pause.

"Oh," Tony continues, "what did you do this weekend, Lawson? Did your prude girlfriend let you kiss her with your tongue yet? I asked you, what did you do this weekend?" Tony presses on.

Liam pauses, awaiting my response. Between the beer bottles and stolen tablets, I feel trapped in a triad of lies.

"Nothing." I respond coldly, looking away from Liam.

"Hey, did you guys hear about North East?" Tony asks, apparently bewildered that he was speaking to the suspects.

"Oh, yeah, someone stole some tablets, right?" I say, a little more emboldened.

Liam gave a little grin as if to say, 'Choose your words carefully.'

"Yeah," Tony says. "But, that's stupid, because they can't even use those tablets, because they probably have passwords."

"They don't use passwords on elementary tablets," Liam says, pretending to be an outsider.

"Yeah, but aren't they like pink and blue kid ones?" Tony asks.

"Maybe, but you can always sell them and take the money," Liam replies.

"Sounds like you know a lot of about this, Liam," Tony says, kidding.

Liam smirks with a tilted head a says, "I would never do something so despicable."

The thought of Liam going to prison or juvie gives me a warm and fuzzy feeling inside. I struggle to see the scared deer analogy in Liam or Tony. Honestly, I only see two jerks with no moral conscience.

Tony hobbles off, leaving me alone with Liam.

"Listen, sh-- head. You're obviously not as cool as I thought. Keep your mouth shut."

"Liam... I looked up to you, but now I feel like you're bullying me."

Liam is irritated, but I continue before he can speak. "I know you're not the starting QB or valedictorian, and I know you don't want to be. You shouldn't, because that's not you. But, neither is this."

Liam looks at me for a second. "So, you think you know me, because we hung out a few times? What are you going to do, tell on me?"

"No... Besides, I'm not perfect. So, I shouldn't be pointing fingers either. I'm just starting over without the fear of doing what's right. What you do is your decision."

I give him a pat on the back and walk away without letting him respond. I feel like I said a lot, but was it too preachy? It sounded like something Brad would want me to say. Hopefully, Liam won't run up from behind me and break my neck, but there are other students around, so he'll probably wait until after school.

I feel terrified and ecstatic. It's a rush, doing what's right when risk is involved. It's kind of like the rush from doing what's wrong like stealing tablets, but better, much better. I have no idea if what I said would help or not, but I don't have any regrets this time.

Lunch rolls around and I find myself sitting with Connor, because, well, I just don't care anymore.

"Hey, I heard what happened between you and Willow..." he says.

"What? From who?"

"Willow."

"So, she broke up with me?" I ask, trying to find out through him.

Connor looks at me, confused, wondering why I said it as a question.

"Well, yeah, but—"

"But, what?" I plead, trying to keep my voice down.

"Well, she is really torn up about it."

"So, what, you're her crying shoulder now?" I ask

defensively.

"You know she doesn't like me like that," he says, wishing she did. "Lawson, you cheated on her. You broke her heart."

"Yeah, I know," I say, staring at my mashed potatoes.

"Why? Why would you cheat on Willow?" he asks, truly befuddled.

"Because, I'm stupid."

"You're not stupid. What you did was stupid, but you did it because you're prideful."

I look up at Connor. He isn't trying to be mean. I can tell he cares about Willow… and me.

"You're right," I say humbly. "I was arrogant."

I take a bite of green beans. "Brad helped set my ways straight the other night," I say. "I know what I need to do, but now I just need to do it."

"Do what?"

"Apologize to her. Try to get her back."

"What if she doesn't want you back?"

I look out at the laughing students around me.

"Well… I'll learn a hard lesson."

"Lawson…" Connor pauses, putting his fork down. "You're one of the most popular students in this school, and you also seem like one of the most miserable students."

I smirk. "I guess popularity isn't such a good thing after all, huh?"

"I don't know. I mean, Char is popular, but she seems

happy." he replies stuffing his face with mashed potatoes.

The first image I see when he says, "Char," is her smiling. He's right. She always seems happy and in a real way.

"So, why is she so happy?" I ask. "Is it because she doesn't cheat and lie?" I let out a flat chuckle.

Connor is in the middle of drinking his chocolate milk. "That's part of it, I think." he adds wiping his milk mustache. "She… well… she seems to care more about people than her popularity. Maybe that's why she's popular. Maybe that's why people like her."

I gnaw at a chicken finger, contemplating my dysfunctional balance between liking people and not liking people.

"And, you actually like me?" I ask Connor without making eye contact.

"Do *you* actually like *me*?" he flips the question on me.

I chuckle, turning toward him. "I didn't like how you volunteered us at the assembly, but I honestly admire your, I don't know, contentment?"

Connor pats me on the back, smiling. "I'll take that as a yes."

"Ha, no, really, I like you Connor. I think I'm seeing that more and more. I just—"

"You wanted popularity, and I wanted friends. There's a difference. That's why I'm happier than you."

"What?" I ask.

"Brad told me it one time. There's a difference between

popularity and friends. Friends make you happy, but popularity doesn't. I have friends." Connor states like it's something everyone knows.

I look at him perplexed.

"Seriously," he adds. "I have you, Willow, Jacob—"

"Who is Jacob?"

"See! You don't even know. Sure, he's not on the football team or student council, but he's a nice guy."

I nod in agreement, turning back to my food. "…You could be making that name up, though."

Connor laughs.

"Look, remember when you asked me on Ned what I want, and I said, 'This.'"

I think for a moment. "Yeah. It was such a beautiful view."

"I wasn't talking about the view." He says with a grin curling on the edge of his mouth.

I tilt my head, trying to understand.

Connor continues. "I was talking about you, having a friend that I could sit with up there."

I plop my fork down in disbelief. "Wait, first of all that's really cheesy, but are you serious?"

"Haha. Yes!"

"Come on, man!"

Connor blushes, slightly embarrassed by his vulnerability.

"Now I really feel like a jerk."

"Good!" Connor teases, reaching for his milk.

I pat Connor on the back. "You know, I—"

Splat!

Something big and wet hits my face and gets into my right eye. I jump back as a reflex and fall out of my seat onto the floor.

I put my hands to my face, wiping off the thick creamy substance from my eyes and nose.

Potatoes. Someone threw potatoes in my face.

My eye stings, but my attention is immediately brought to my wrist. I must have hurt it trying to catch my fall.

People are laughing. I want to light all their hair on fire, but at the same time, this feels like what I deserve. I get up and look in the direction of where it came from to see who threw it. People are laughing harder now, because I guess buttermilk mashed potatoes paint my face and hair like a Halloween costume. I hold my wrist in pain. A girl looks at me like she is sorry for me but isn't about to say anything. Who could have done this? Surely, Willow isn't that mad at me. Tony? Liam? There's only one person sick and twisted enough to do such a thing.

I scan the cafeteria in the direction it came from until I find her. Yup, the deep creased furrow. Britney. She sits at the table in front of me, grinning at me like a gargoyle with laughing trolls at her side. They go back to eating, trying to pretend they know nothing. I know it's not right to hit a girl, but what if she's evil and is equally as strong as you? Yeah, I know violence is not the answer. I grab a napkin from the table to wipe my face, thinking about my next move. Literally… maybe I will move out of this town.

"*Agghhh!*"

I look up to see Britney's entire head covered in ketchup and her friends also have a good portion on their pretty little outfits.

Sydney.

Sydney stands above Britney with an entire tub of ketchup, the kind you pump, now emptied out on Britney's hair.

Now, the entire cafeteria is focused on this full-out drama.

Sydney stands on the table shouting, "I am not in love with Lawson, and bullying is bad!" She points down at Britney and tosses the ketchup tub across the room.

The security guard rushes in to escort Sydney off as she throws a middle finger in the air.

Maybe not the approach I was thinking, and definitely not the person, but I appreciate the effort.

Britney frantically tries to clean herself off. She looks sad and embarrassed, and then I see it: the scared deer. I grab an entire tray of napkins and walk over to her. All eyes in the cafeteria are on me. Without saying anything, I hand napkins to her friends and start cleaning her off. She doesn't know what to do at first, but before she can tell me no, I hold out a napkin.

"Hey, I'm sorry I hurt your knee, and I'm sorry Sydney

threw ketchup on you. Can we be friends now?"

She freezes, not knowing what to say, as if no one has ever shown her true kindness before. I throw my arms around her, giving her no choice. Slowly, she puts her arms around me, and people start cheering. I think a lunch lady is even tearing up to my right.

We both laugh as we clean up our little food fight. Of course, we get escorted into the principal's office to meet with Sydney, because no matter how it ends, I guess throwing potatoes and ketchup is never acceptable.

"Sit down you two," Dr. Novak commands from behind his desk. Sydney is already sitting in one of the chairs next to the wall. She gives me a subtle wink. Britney and I look like we murdered someone from the ketchup, and I'm sure there is still potato substance somewhere on the region of my face.

"Obviously, this school has a policy against throwing food, which can lead to detention and even suspension. Now," Dr. Novak says looking at me and Britney. "This is my second meeting regarding the two of you lately. Being the case, my typical response to this would be automatic suspension."

My eyes widen. Suspension means I can't play football, and my dad would kill me.

"But, based on eye-witnesses from the cafeteria, I heard you two had an unusual moment of reconciliation initiated by you, Mr. Peters." Dr. Novak's eyes soften for the first time. "We need more behavior like that at this school. And, apparently Mr. Peter's peace offering was received, yes?" he asks Britney.

Britney nods revealing the slightest smile.

"And you miss," Dr. Novak says turning toward Sydney. "Inexcusable, what you did. Bullying does not permit bullying. What would you like to say to Britney?"

Sydney pushes her black bangs behind her ear and gave Britney the nicest patronizing smile possible. "Sorry, Britney. I shouldn't have done that, and it seems like Lawson didn't need my help anyway."

"It's OK," Britney says in a tone I actually believe. "And, something else…" Britney says looking at me and then back at Dr. Novak. "I made those election posters that got Lawson in trouble… I'm sorry."

"Wow, I'm impressed by your courage and honest remorse Britney," Dr. Novak says raising his eyebrows.

Dr. Novak leans back in his chair and crosses his arms with one hand rubbing his chin. A smirk slowly forms on lips as he rocks back and forth. "I'm impressed with how mature you all are handling this even though your actions were childish. This is a final warning, and future events will lead to suspension. Now, go clean yourselves up. You're excused." Dr. Novak's smirk dissolves into his 'business as usual' expression followed by us scurrying to freedom.

My wrist still hurts. I had to go to the nurse, and she thinks I might have sprained it. Oh, and it's my right hand, so there goes football for a while. The weird thing is that I'm not mad. I'm just happy that Britney and I are now friends. Ha, I guess Gabe finally gets his dream of playing quarterback.

Connor stops me in the hall. "Proud of you, man," he says, nodding. "What you did in there was pretty amazing. Here... Willow wanted me to give you this." He holds out a note.

"What does it say?"

"I don't know."

I gave him a look.

"Seriously! I mean, I really wanted to look, but I didn't. You do know that you two are, like, the only people in the school who write love notes on real paper."

I take the note and open it, noticing Connor is still standing there.

"You don't have to tell me, but you can if you want," Connor says, leeching onto me.

"Lawson," the letter reads. "I'm proud of what you did at lunch. I always knew there was an amazing guy inside of you. We can be friends, but I'm not ready for anything more at this time."

I look up at Connor, grinning.

I shake my head. "Just friends... at this time," I say, making quotations marks with my fingers.

"Thank goodness, the drama has been killing me. I hope

the rest of high school isn't like this. You're a stressful friend you know that?" he says.

"ME? YOU... you... oh, it's not even worth it." I say, throwing my hands in the air.

"You get your math homework done?" Connor asks as we walk to class.

"Yeah, I copied off your mom."

"People don't say that anymore."

I like to take credit for turning Connor into a semi-funny person. After school, I had to face the coaches about being put on the disability list by mashed potatoes. Tony is happy that I'm hurt, even though he didn't say it. It's like we are even again. Gabe is completely freaked out in both a good and bad way. The team freaked out, too. They basically ran the ball every play, and Gabe got smashed on a sack at one point, which I think was intentional by the offensive line.

I feel pretty good about my life... except for my home life. I wonder what Dad is going to do and how mom is managing. All the events of the day have taken my mind off the fact that we might have to sell our house. It's weird, though, because I feel like this is a time when a child would need his parents, but the truth is, they need me.

During practice, Tony and I avoid each other, but I know need to say something. Even though Tony is a jerk, I don't want to turn into him. After practice, I walk up to him.

"I'm sorry." I say, standing in front of him.

Tony smirks and zips up his bag.

"Tony."

Tony looks up to me with a sneer.

"Seriously, I'm not apologizing because I'm afraid of you. I'm apologizing, because what I said was wrong. I got cocky, because of all that has happened to me. The truth is that you are the better quarterback, and you should be proud of that."

Tony's eyes soften.

"I know … but …thanks. And umm…" He struggles finding his words.

"The truth is… Well, look, I've had a lot going on lately."

"What do you mean?" I ask.

Tony looks at me. "My stepdad is an asshole, OK? He's always drunk, and the last couple weeks he's been messin' with my mom."

"Messin' with your Mom?"

"He's been hitting her, OK? And… well, I know I'm a better QB than you," he says, smirking. "That's not what I'm jealous about."

I look at him, confused. "What?"

"Dude, you have normal parents who aren't divorced or doped out."

I start laughing.

"What?" he asks, confused.

"My mom is depressed and on medication, and my dad just lost his job and has an anger problem."

"So, your life isn't perfect either, huh?" Tony asks, smiling.

I shake my head. "All this time, I thought it was about me. I didn't know you were going through that. But, hey, if your stepdad is hitting your mom, you need to call social services or something."

"Already did," Tony says, smiling. "You're a good man, Laws."

I extend my fist.

"We cool?"

Tony nods and pounds my knuckles. "Cool."

I leave the fieldhouse shaking my head. I can't believe how wrong my thinking had been and how quick I assumed and judged. Like Brad said, everyone wants something. I thought Tony just wanted to be cool, when actually, he just wants a family. I guess the same is true for me. I just want my family back. I scan the parking lot, looking for my dad's truck, but I don't see it.

Honk!

It's my mom's car. What is she doing here? I get in to see her beaming smile.

"Hey… Mom, wow, you seem to be in a good mood. Where's Dad?"

"Well, sweetie, I am feeling much better."

"Wh— how? A different medication?"

"Same medication, but I've also went on an elimination diet, you know, where you cut out sugar, wheat, dairy…"

"Geez, what's left?"

"Ha, well, fruit, vegetables, meat, potatoes, and nuts. Anyway, I'm feeling much better, and I think gluten has been causing most of my depression."

"Gluten, as in bread?"

"Yeah, and pasta, cakes, and anything with flour. I read that some people are fine with it, but others are sensitive, even allergic, and even other people can get depression and stuff from it, like me."

"Wait, what's that smell?" I ask, getting a strong whiff. "Is that Ch—"

"CHINESE FOOD!" Dad says, popping up from the backseat.

"Geez, Dad, you... GEEZ, you almost gave me a heart attack! What's going on?" I ask, trying to get a grip on reality.

"Honey, do you want to tell him?" Mom asks Dad.

"There's been a change of events," he says.

"Change of events?" I ask.

"Yeah, it was found out that my boss has been under the influence on the job, and he hit an employee yesterday over the head with a clip board, so upper management fired him. Well, the new boss is much nicer, and after reviewing my folder and hearing from coworkers, they've decided to give me a second chance!" Dad says with new life in his eyes.

"That's awesome, Dad! So, you're keeping your job!"

"I'm not fired!" Dad has never seemed happier. He hands

out the food, and we eat while still parked.

"So, does your food have gluten, Mom?"

"Not the Beef and Broccoli. They use gluten-free soy sauce."

I take a bite of my General Tso's Chicken, and a feeling of bliss overtakes me. Maybe it is the Chinese food, or maybe it is the feeling of having my family back, but it feels good. For the first time since I moved here, everything—this school, my family, and my life—feel not perfect but... good.

I tell them about my whole day from the break up to the food fight to the sprained wrist. Mom is concerned about me getting into a fight, even though it was a food fight with a girl, but Dad gets a kick out of it. I tell them I am OK with it all, and they say they are proud of me.

When we get home, I decide to tell Brad the good news.

"I'm going to talk with Brad. I'll be back in a while."

"OK, sweetie. Have fun," Mom replies as Dad is still stuffing his face with lo mein noodles while trying to open the front door. As I approach Brad's house, I notice him sitting on the grass in his backyard.

Brad flashes a big, loving smile. "Lawson! Come sit with me. It's a beautiful day."

"Yes, it is!" I say, plopping down next to him.

"Wow," Brad says, lifting his sunglasses to get a better look at me. "What happened today?"

"Ha, everything..."

I tell him the whole story, from how I handled Liam and Tony to how Connor and I are friends again to the lunch food fight. Brad doesn't respond much. I think he is taking it all in like a proud pseudo father trying to hold the tears back.

"Brad," I say, needing to admit something. "You were right about me wanting to be popular. I didn't want to be left out and become a nobody."

Brad leans back on his elbows. "You're anything but a nobody," he says looking at me through his sunglasses. "So, what do you want now?"

I look out at the green grass, smiling. "I want more days like today."

"Lawson… you don't know how proud I am of you," Brad says, looking over his knees and down the hill to the woods.

"Well… you had a lot to do with that," I say, elbowing him in the knee. "Thank you."

I can tell Brad is starting to get choked up, but his sunglasses still cover his eyes.

"So," I say, "what are you up to now?"

Brad pauses, looks up at the sky and then finally takes off his glasses.

"Lawson, I'm moving."

The smile on my face drops. "What?"

"I'm moving."

"Why? Where?"

"Oregon. My mom lives there, and she's not doing well.

She's getting old, and she needs my help. Besides, I need to move on from this house, and I think I've found my closure."

"But, I'll never get to see you!" I say, coming to grips with what he is saying.

"Lawson, I'm so sorry. You and Connor are my favorite things about this place, and it's hard for me to leave, but I've been neglecting my mom for too long, and if I'm not there for her when she needs me the most... I... I need to do this. I want to do this."

I sit in disbelief.

"There's something else I want to tell you," he says, turning to me. "I thought a lot about what you said the other night about me forgiving the guy who hit my wife and daughter..." Brad looks away for a second. "I'm going to visit him on my way out and make my peace. Even if he doesn't deserve it, I need it. I need to let go. And, I bet he needs it too. The people who deserve love the least need it the most."

"But... who is going to teach me if you leave?"

"Well, I suppose we could Skype and email, but you're empowered now, so it's time you start empowering others, and it sounds like you're already doing that. Help others becomes leaders. You'll keep learning, even if it's not from me. Just make sure whoever moves in this house keeps this grass looking good," Brad says, trying to cut the tension.

"I'm going to miss you, Brad. You've been like a father to

me."

Brad struggles to hold it in.

"And you like a son to me. But, you have a father, and you two need each other. You need to spend more time with him. I bet there's a lot you don't know about each other."

Brad stands, shaking off his pants.

"You and Connor look after each other, and Willow too for that matter." He sticks his hand out for me to shake.

"I'm proud of you, Lawson."

I throw my arms around him like he's my dad. He must have been startled, because we never hugged before, but I don't care. He slowly wraps his arms around me in a big embrace. "Thank you, Lawso—" He struggles getting the words out as they choked up in his throat.

"Thank you for helping me face my enemy," I say, holding onto him.

Brad pats my back. "Back at you."

Brad gives one final pat on my shoulder and turns toward his house. "You know what I see in you, Lawson?"

"What?" I ask.

He smirks, "Freshman Wisdom."

"But, wait. Isn't that an oxymoron? I thought freshmen are known for not being wise."

"True, but wisdom comes to those who seek it... no matter the age. Take care, Lawson."

Brad smiles and disappears into his house.

The clouds roll across the sky as a warm breeze touches my face. I'm going to miss Brad. He is like another father to me. I look around at all the cookie-cutter houses and remember how I had imagined a giant setting them up like Monopoly houses. Maybe it wasn't a giant. Maybe it was God. Yeah, it must be God, because a giant wouldn't be that smart, and he wouldn't care that much. Thanks for putting Brad here, God. He was perfectly placed.

God responds with a steady breeze and the sound of a train in the distance.

Chapter 15

"I'm going to the pool, Mom!" I yell, walking out the front door into the bright midday sun.

June.

Summer.

Being a freshman was kind of crazy, really. It's so different than middle school. So, let me catch you up on the last eight months. It's been a wild ride... but worth it. Where do I start? Well, I won Homecoming King, yeah, so, that happened! Guess who my date was. Nope, not Willow. Not even Sydney. Yup, Britney! As friends, of course; turns out she really is strong, because at one point she picked me up and swung me around. Sure, I was annoyed and emasculated but also impressed. Liam finally came around and turned himself in for the tablets. I'm not sure what his punishment was, but it included community service. I'm not sure if he confessed because he knew he would get caught eventually or if he had a change of heart. Either way, I stopped hanging out with him. Sure, I lost some friends, but not the ones that matter. Our football season was kind of a dud, because it took me a while to heal, but Gabe tried his best. He was excited when

I took over again. He said he won't be playing next year and, instead, he's trying out for golf. Tony healed just in time to play the last game. Coach put him back as QB, and I went back to wide receiver. We still lost, but he was happy. The coaches never found out about the beer bottles, and yes, Tony definitely still drinks, but not as much. One step at a time, I guess. His stepdad is out of the picture, and his mom is doing better.

Basketball season was good, but I'm not starting. I had to sit the bench but still got decent playing time. So, it's all good. Besides, I have three more years. Connor tried out for the school play, and it turns out he's quite the actor. Ironically, he played The Cowardly Lion in The Wizard of Oz. Brad would be proud, because Connor finally found his courage.

Speaking of Brad, he stuck to his word and moved to Oregon, but not before visiting the Leavenworth Prison. He said he sat in his car for one hour before forcing himself to go in. The person who killed Brad's wife and daughter is a 44-year-old guy named Justin. He wasn't drunk when he was driving... but he was texting. He was already kind of messed up from life, I guess, but that accident sent him over the edge. He tried killing himself in prison, twice. When Brad showed up, he said Justin looked scared, like he was expecting Brad to cuss him out, but Brad took a play from his own playbook and chose forgiveness. He actually mentored Justin for one week before moving, and now Justin leads a 'Loving Leadership' group in the prison. Oh, and it includes a certain green book about a boy and a tree.

My mom and dad? They're doing good. Maybe too good, because I guess they've gotten closer in their marriage and now they're always all over each other. It's kind of gross, but I love them. Also, we're going to church, the same one Connor goes to. It has helped our family. My dad and I have grown closer to each other, and yes, he still says, 'Dude.' Plus, our cabinet is full of gluten-free things, and Mom started a blog on 'How Food Affects Your Brain.'

So, life is good for me, now. I'm still popular at school, not because of the parties I go to, but because I'm nice to people. I've learned that being popular is not bad. The problem is when you think it will make you happy. Having a few good friends is worth more than a bunch of fake ones.

There are only a few people at the pool today, a grandma and her grandkids and a pretty girl lying in the corner. Hmm, where should I sit? I choose the pretty girl. Besides, I think she likes me.

"Hey, babe!" I say, walking over to her.

She twirls her straight blonde hair and chewing gum with her eyes shaded by big brown sunglasses. Looking up from her book, she smirks and motions for me to sit next to her.

"Are you new here?" I ask nonchalantly.

"Um… well… if you want me to be," she says, batting

her eyes at me. "Don't you have a cute friend you hang out with?" she asks.

"Connor?"

"Yeah… Connor."

"You like him?"

"Yeah… but I like you more."

Willow puts her book back over her face.

Oh, yeah, Willow and I got back together. Duh! Did you have any doubt? She's kind of awesome. We're basically going to get married someday, but we don't talk about it, yet, because that would make things awkward.

So, here I am, a kid who thought that moving was the worst thing that could happen to him, but it turned out to be the best. Maybe it was fate, or maybe it was coincidence. Maybe it was a dorky kid at a pool, an intriguing guy down the street, and an amazing girl in a coffee shop. Maybe. Maybe it's not what happens to you as much as who is in your life as it happens.

I learned a lot in my freshman year. I learned that, like a paradox, some things don't make sense at first until you see them through. Just because something is tough doesn't mean it's bad. I learned to love the tough, not for what it is, but for what it made me, tougher. I learned that the more love you give, the more love you have. I learned that leadership is doing what you know is right, with what you know you can do, to help others with what they think they can't do. And,

I learned that our biggest enemy is often ourselves. I also learned that mashed potatoes can sting for a long time if they get in your eyes, and I learned that giving someone a second chance is always worth it.

The sun glistens off the rippling pool like liquid jewelry. I look over at Brad's house, well, his old house. I imagine Brad's blue Durango in the driveway and him carrying milk inside, listening to his earbuds. My daydream fades, and a white car replaces the Durango. A new family lives there now, but I don't know them. They have a middle school boy and a little girl, and they both seem like little terrors. In fact, here they come now. The boy is chasing his sister out the house as they rip a path toward the pool carrying toys and a ball in both arms. The girl has a wild-eyed expression that suggests you shouldn't let the red pig tails fool you. How do parents even do it?

They bolt through the pool gate, and they pick on each other about the toys, or something. Mom and dad are nowhere to be seen, and I'm not planning on babysitting. Willow seems unfazed and glued to her book. The little girl is a rascal, but the boy is definitely on a whole other level. He is short and stocky with a blond buzz cut and freckles. He grabs her toys and runs toward us, jumping with all the toys into the pool making a huge splash. The little girl has floaties on her arms and jumps in after him, yelling the whole way. Now, they are full-out splashing, which I wouldn't care if not for the water getting on me, not to mention the high-pitched whinny noises that make you want to blow a fog horn in someone's face.

I can't take it anymore.

"Hey!" I say, sitting up. "Stop splashing!"

The boy looks at me with a smirk that I want to wipe away using the bottom of the pool. "You're not my dad. Why should I listen to you?"

He has a good point, and I feel sorry for his dad, but then I notice the ball they brought. It's a football.

"Do you play football?" I ask.

He looks at the ball and then back at me. "Yeah, I'll be a seventh grader and plan on playing quarterback next year."

"Are you good?"

"Yeah," he says with a cocky little grin.

My annoyance rises as I imagine living next to these two for the next three years. How can someone be so arrogant? He's just a little punk bully who thinks he's all that, but he's probably just—I catch myself mid-thought as I stare into the darkness of his eyes reflecting back to me. The kid reminds me of someone. A familiarity I know well. He's probably just… like… me.

The kid is me. Me, one year ago. He's afraid of moving. He's afraid of not being liked in a new school, of not starting football. He's covering it all up with sarcasm, but he's just a scared deer. As I see him, I see me, and I see what Brad saw.

Opportunity.

"No, you're not," I say, matching his cockiness.

"What?"

"I said, 'no, you're not.'"

"Yes, I am!"

"OK, prove it. Throw me the ball," I say, standing up.

"Why?"

"Because, I don't think you can."

His face grimaces like he wants to kill me using the football. He grabs the ball and launches it at me. It isn't a bad throw but a little low.

I pick up the ball. Pointing it toward his house, I launch the ball into the sky. It flies with a perfect spiral up over the pool fence all the way into his driveway. His eyes get as big as his ego, and his mouth drops open in shock.

"I was the freshman quarterback, and by the time you're in high school, I'll be varsity."

He looks at the ball bouncing around in his driveway and then back at me. I can tell his confidence is not a big as his mouth. He doesn't know what to say. I can see the scared deer inside him, and I thought of Brad's words. 'Do what you know is right with what you know you can do to help others with what they think they can't do.'

"I'm going to train you this summer."

His face softens. "Really?"

"Yeah, and I bet you'll not only be playing this year. I bet you'll be starting."

"Why do you think that?"

"Because, I'm going to teach you. I'm going to teach you how to do more than play football. I'm going to show you how to be a leader."

His eyes light up, and his guard comes down.

"Now," I say, unable to keep a straight face. "Let's go talk about your yard."

He gets out of the pool with his sister following behind. "Oh, and I'm bringing a friend over. He's kind of a dork, but you're gonna love him."

I make my way over to the house like I've done numerous times before, but this time is different. This time, I am going to do the teaching.

"Hey, are you afraid of heights?" I ask.

"No, why?"

"Because we're going to climb a tree, and I'm going to teach you stuff."

"What stuff?"

"Freshman wisdom."

We are who we choose to be over time.